UGLY AS
SIN

PRAISE FOR *UGLY AS SIN*

"*Ugly As Sin* is James Newman's best book yet! I loved every brutal, violent, pulpy page, and I recommend the hell out of it!"

—**Jeff Strand**, Author of *Dead Clown Barbecue*, *Faint of Heart*, and *Gleefully Macabre Tales*

"*Ugly As Sin* is a terrific page-turner, a body slam of a book that features tough-guy noir, freakish horrors, and human redemption. James Newman skillfully spins a spiral of suspense that pulls you in and won't let go."

—**Brian Pinkerton**, Author of *Killer's Diary*, *Rough Cut*, and *How I Started the Apocalypse*

"*Ugly As Sin* is brutal, fast-paced, grimy fun, a compulsive page-turner with characters you'll be deeply invested in by story's end."

—**Blu Gilliand**, *October Country*

"*Ugly As Sin* has about as vicious a premise as I've ever come across. It's not what it first appears to be. It's worse. Wrapped inside its mystery and ticking-clock hunt is the most jaundiced indictment possible of the corrupted soul of celebrity culture...its feeders and especially its fed."

—**Brian Hodge**, Author of *Picking the Bones* and *Whom the Gods Would Destroy*

"James Newman is one of my favorite authors. His novels are always engrossing and entertaining. I can't recommend his works highly enough."

—**John Little**, Author of *Miranda*, *The Memory Tree*, and *Ursa Major*

Also by James Newman

Holy Rollers

Midnight Rain

The Wicked

The Forum

Revenge Flick!

Animosity

Olden

Collaborations

Night of the Loving Dead
(with James Futch)

Death Songs from the Naked Man
(with Donn Gash)

Love Bites
(with Donn Gash)

The Church of Dead Languages
(with Jason Brannon)

Collections

People Are Strange

Previously published in limited edition hardcover
by Thunderstorm books and trade paperback by Shock Totem Publications.

This edition has been revised and expanded.

Cover art by Mikio Murakami
Cover type design by Yannick Bouchard
Layout by K. Allen Wood

Copyright © 2017 by Apex Publications, LLC

www.apexbookcompany.com

ISBN 978-1-937009-50-2

UGLY AS SIN

A NOVEL OF WHITE-TRASH NOIR

JAMES NEWMAN

Lexington, KY

This one's for DAD. Through the years, as you taught me what it means to be a man, I might have thought you were a "heel" at times...but you've always been the good guy.

I hope I make you proud. I love you.

They caught him walking out the back door of the Amarillo Civic Center around one a.m. At six foot nine, a hair under three hundred pounds, he was the biggest in the Biz. But a homerun whack to the back of his skull with their aluminum baseball bat was enough to lay the giant down.

Of course, what fun would it have been if they stopped there?

Motherfuckers hit him again, in the ribs.

A third time, across his bum knee, for shits and giggles.

Then everything went black for Nick Bullman, a.k.a. The Widowmaker.

†

"Wake up, asshole."

A high-pitched titter, like the mating call of some brain-damaged bird, followed by a second voice: "Time to pay the piper!"

"Shit, that smarts," Nick groaned as he came to.

At least one of his ribs was broken, he knew right away—he could feel it scraping against something soft and vital inside of him with every breath he took. His head throbbed as if an eighteen-wheeler had rammed into it at full speed. Not to mention his left knee. Damn thing hadn't been the same since Harry Hardcore's sloppy Figure Four at the Brawler Series last summer. Now it felt as if that same eighteen-wheeler had driven over it, reversed, did it a few more times to add insult to injury.

Once he was fully conscious, Nick went to rub at the back of his head. But he couldn't move. His captors had cuffed his wrists together behind some sort of steel post. He looked down to see that his ankles were bound as well, with black rubber bungee cords.

The persons responsible for his predicament were fuzzy humanoid shapes at first, looming twenty or thirty feet away from him. They watched Nick struggle and flex and curse their mommas for a minute before they stepped closer...

Two men. About half his age, but a thousand times uglier. The first thing Nick noticed: they wore matching referee shirts. Zebra-striped, zip-up, the Association's blood-splatter logo on the left breast. Guy on the right, the taller of the two, sported maybe half as many teeth in his mouth as Nick had fingers and toes. Tufts of dirty blond hair stuck out from under his Longhorns baseball cap. On the T-shirt beneath his rumpled ref-wear, Nick recognized a smirking portrait of Rebel Yell, those Confederate Flag-wearing "rednecks" whose gimmick portrayed them as tag-team spokesmen for the downtrodden Southern man. Guy on the left had a few more teeth than his companion, but only one arm—the other ended at his elbow in a pink, misshapen knob. A tangled mop of curly brown hair fell just past his shoulders. The shirt beneath One-Arm's ref-wear advertised his idolization for the Association's reigning Heavyweight Champ, Big Bubba Bad-Ass.

Nick sat in one corner of what looked like a homemade wrestling ring. The thick blackness beyond it and a hint of corrugated metal suggested some kind of warehouse. Rust-colored splotches stained the mat beneath his feet. Even the smell was authentic: sweat, baby oil, and soggy spandex.

Nick was almost impressed. To suggest that the men before him were wrestling fans was like saying...well, like saying the matches were choreographed and it was all a soap opera for dudes.

"Here's the deal, Mr. Widowmaker," the guy in the Rebel Yell shirt began the festivities. He stood over Nick, arms crossed. "There was a time when people liked you. You seemed like a decent fella. But then I don't know what happened. You got too big for your britches, betrayed your buddies in the Alliance. I couldn't believe it when you hit Joe Cobra with that steel chair. You helped Garth Hater take the one-two-three, left your buddies high n' dry. After all you guys had been through!"

"With friends like you," spat One-Arm, "who needs enemies."

"That was ten years ago." Even as he said it, Nick wondered why he was explaining himself to these freaks. "Ratings had dropped. McDougal wanted to shake things up."

"You oughta be ashamed o' yourself," said Rebel Yell. His tongue raked across his rotten teeth as he spoke, and the sound was like a snake slithering across wet concrete. "Them guys was your *best friends*! Scotty Mojo, Freddy Face, even that wetback, El Diablo. They believed that horseshit about the Corporation brain-washin' you. Remember when you was gonna give away Freddy's fiancée? They was tyin' the knot at *Doomsday XVII*, right before Diablo's 'Rage In the Cage' match with Vesuvius. But you turned on your buddies, and you hit Miss Jessica with the ring-bell?"

One-Arm nodded, his single skinny limb flailing about as if to emphasize his buddy's point. "What the hell's wrong with you? Always kickin' below the belt, cheatin' to win. It ain't right!"

"I'm on one of those hidden camera shows, right? Is that what's going on here?" Nick no longer knew whether to laugh or fear for his life. This felt like a lame beginning to an even lamer storyline, something the Association's writers had conjured up on the fly but they had neglected to tell him about it. Marks who believed the work was *real*? Thirty, forty years ago maybe. But wasn't it common knowledge these days that the outcome of every match was predetermined, and even the promoters called what he did for a living "sports entertainment"?

Apparently, these two morons didn't get out much.

"You think you're so smart," said Rebel Yell. "But we got you! Waited on you after the main event, almost didn't recognize you without your demonistic makeup."

"We *got* you," One-Arm said. "Fucker."

Without warning, Rebel Yell reared back and slugged Nick in the mouth.

Nick hadn't noticed the guy's glove before now. It was one of those steel-lined SAP jobs. Often used by law enforcement, designed to inflict maximum damage.

His busted lip leaked blood down his chin. He spat out a tooth.

Still, he couldn't help the chuckle that slipped out of him. "Stupid marks. You don't even deserve to wash my cup."

"Look," said Rebel Yell, as if trying to reason with the wrestler before things *really* got out of hand, "When Black Samson killed you in that 'Loser Leaves Life' match at *New Year's Evil IX*, what'd you do?"

Nick decided to play along. Why not. He had nowhere else to be. "I didn't *do* anything, right? I was *dead*."

"Big Bubba carried you backstage, told the crowd he was gonna do what was right since you two used to be close. Said he was gonna talk Father Ivan Ruffstuff into givin' you a proper Christian burial."

"But then you sold your soul to Moloch so you could live forever! A week later, on *Thursday Night Hardcore*, how did you repay Big Bubba?"

"Don't recall. But I'm sure you'll refresh my memory."

"You slammed him through the entrance ramp, you asshole! You teamed up with the guy who slit your throat, helped that nigger throw Bubba *fifteen feet* onto the concrete floor. You broke his back!"

When Rebel Yell was done, he looked like he might start crying.

Truth told, Nick had always liked Big Bubba—this past 4th of July, in fact, their families had gotten together for a barbecue in Mr. Bad-Ass's (real name: Eric Aubrey) backyard, Nick pushing Aubrey's giggling eleven-year-old on her swing-set, harmlessly flirting with Mrs. Bubba as he was wont to do—though things appeared quite the opposite inside the squared circle.

In the ring, their ongoing feud kept the fans screaming for blood. Usually the Widowmaker's.

After all, Nick Bullman was the GWA's top heel. All that sacrilege, cartoonish crap about 'Maker being the SON OF ETERNAL DARKNESS—it never failed to get the marks going good.

"Actually," said Nick, "Eric had some vacation time to burn, took Renee to the Bahamas for their anniversary…"

He trailed off. Knew it was like trying to argue with a couple of ring-posts.

"Sure. We messed Big Bubba up good. Put his ass in ICU."

"You're *evil*, Mr. Widowmaker," said Rebel Yell. "You've bullied your way through the Global Wrestling Association long enough."

He pronounced it *rasslin'*. Naturally.

"You're worse than Leviathan!" said One-Arm. "At least he's a big dumb monster, can't help doin' the things he does."

Nick shook his head. This had to be some surreal steroid dream. But then, he hadn't touched the juice for the better part of three decades.

"You dildos are crazier than my third wife," he said. "And trust me, that's pretty fucking crazy."

Rebel Yell reached into his ref shirt. Gripped something hidden between his pants and the small of his back. He brought it out.

The knife was one of those big mean sons-a-bitches with a serrated blade, spiked knuckle guard. Kinda piece made you feel like you should start bleeding somewhere tender just for looking at it. It reminded Nick of a weapon from some post-apocalyptic B-movie, something with leather-clad road warriors and mutants running amok.

"You do it," Rebel Yell told One-Arm. "I'll hold him."

His companion nodded, let loose with another birdlike giggle as if he had waited his whole life for this moment. Rebel Yell scrabbled like a spider atop the ring-post to which Nick was cuffed.

A thick rope looped tight around the wrestler's neck, pulling his head back against the turnbuckle.

"You wanna reveal a man's true colors, you gotta dig deep," Rebel Yell whispered into Nick's ear. "Get to the skull beneath the skin."

One-Arm began to cut.

†

Later. Impossible to tell how *much* later, as time—reality—had become a nonsensical joke that was anything but funny.

A cacophony of wailing sirens, doors being kicked in, the staccato clicking of numerous gun-hammers.

"Drop the knife, dirtbag!" someone shouted.

Another voice: "Step away from him! Both of you! *Now!*"

In the center of the chaos: the body of a sweat-soaked muscleman transformed into a bug-eyed Halloween decoration.

"Took you long enough," said the thing in the ring, to the boys in blue standing over it.

More stunned gasps from his saviors, a chorus of disbelief exhaled on breaths that stank of coffee and doughnuts.

Until he spoke, none of them had known he was alive. His massive chest rose and fell so slowly it barely moved at all.

And the blood...so much blood, everywhere they looked...

One tall cop with a 70s-porn-flick moustache slipped on something as he stepped into the ring. He pirouetted gracelessly but caught himself just in time, gripping the top rope with one hand to regain his balance.

A self-conscious glance at his companions. He bent, lifted something pink and dripping from beneath his shiny black shoe.

"Holy Mother of God. Is this what I think—"

He dropped it. It hit the canvas with a sick *plop*.

The policeman looked ready to lose his supper. All of them did.

Nick Bullman stared at the gory pile too. And when some helpful soul finally got around to uncuffing his hands, he reached for it. Wept for it. As if he could just slide it back into place and everything would be A-OK.

Three years later…

He still dreams about it now and then, but more often than not he dreams of what happened after it was over. The repercussions of that night he spent with two men he would always think of—despite having learned their real names in the days following his ordeal—as "Rebel Yell" and "One-Arm."

He dreams of what came *later*. After his tormentors were convicted and sent away. After the surgeons had done their best to fix him.

He dreams of all he has lost.

And strangely enough, he often wakes up smiling...

†

In his dreams, it is that fateful day in late August. He's visiting corporate headquarters in Wilmington, North Carolina for the first (and last) time since Doc Saldutti gave him the OK to return to work. He has already made his rounds, thanking everyone for their awkward *welcome backs* and *good to see yas*. Now his well-wishers have returned to their pencil-pushing and their keyboard-tapping, and Nick finds himself alone at last. He stands at the far end of the hall from the executive hustle and bustle, head down, waiting for the elevator. He doesn't know that, in the coming months, his loneliness will drown him in a sea of black depression. So he welcomes this moment of introspection after playing the role of circus freak surrounded by the gawking masses, folks who pretend to pity him while rejoicing inside: *Poor bastard, sure glad that ain't me.*

Now he's approached by Veronica Townsend, the administrative assistant with the horn-rimmed glasses and the perfect bronze legs that stretch into infinity. Nick turns to her with a distracted frown. Of course, these days he always looks like he's frowning.

When their eyes meet, Ronnie quickly glances down at her clipboard. There's a hitch in her voice, as if she ate some bad fish for lunch: "The, uh, boss wants to see you in his office. ASAP."

Message relayed, she makes her escape. The trail of expensive perfume she leaves in her wake tickles the Widowmaker's nose.

He stomps down the hall to McDougal's office.

As he goes, he pulls out an old yellow handkerchief he keeps in the ass pocket of his jeans. He dabs at the wetness that constantly trickles from his right eye, a result of permanent damage to his tear ducts.

Once the rag is back in his pocket, his huge fist knocks three times on the boss's door, rattling the gold nameplate there: LANCE K.

He waits, careful not to look at his reflection in the nameplate.

He's preparing to knock again when the boss calls out: "Come in!"

Nick pushes the door open. Stoops to clear the threshold.

It's an icebox in here. AC's cranked to full-blast. The room smells like pine-scented Lysol.

The boss is on the phone. Arguing with somebody about how he owns the trademark to every name on the roster so you bet your ass he expects fifty percent of the cut, assuming this piece-of-shit movie gets a green-light in the first place.

When McDougal finally hangs up the phone, Nick wastes no time asking, "You wanted to see me, boss?"

"Nick Bullman." The CEO's teeth are impossibly white. A used car salesman's grin on the face of a filthy rich entertainment mogul. "Take a seat. Please."

Nick eases his six-foot-nine bulk into the chair opposite his employer's mahogany desk. The vinyl cushion is as soft as a boulder beneath his ass. Nick has always wondered if guys like Lance McDougal intentionally stock their offices with furniture only slightly more comfortable than instruments of torture. Just so there's no mistake who has the best seat in the room.

Lance K. McDougal III is in his late forties, just seven or eight years younger than Nick, but being born with the proverbial silver spoon in your kisser tends to slow the aging process. He could pass for thirty-something if not for his hair—it is the color of needles and razorblades, objects that will slice you to pieces if you aren't careful with them. He wears an immaculate navy blue suit, a tie the color of freshly-spilled blood. At barely 5' 5", McDougal is shorter than anyone who works in his building, but thanks to the power he wields as Chief Executive Officer of the Global Wrestling Association the man is no less imposing than the sixty-plus musclemen on his payroll. He inherited the company from his father after Lance K. McDougal, Jr. succumbed to a short battle with lung cancer. The boss's daddy had been a devout Southern Baptist; under his thumb, the Association had produced nothing so controversial as to threaten its Saturday afternoon TV time slot. Now, Lance K. McDougal III has body-slammed sports entertainment into the new millennium, with flamboyant characters and titillating scenarios that barely slip past Standards & Practices week after week.

"Good to see you, Nick," McDougal says. "We were all worried sick

18   UGLY AS SIN

for a while."

"I appreciate that," says Nick.

"Look at you. The doctors...they tried. I'll give them that."

Nick fidgets in his chair. It creaks beneath his weight. He doesn't dig the way McDougal sits there scrutinizing his ruined features, as if they are some abstract work of art on which the boss is thinking about dropping thirty or forty grand.

"I heard some clutz cop actually *stepped on* your face? Jesus."

Nick stares down at his snakeskin boots.

"So how are you feeling, Nick? Ready to get back to work?"

"I'm itching to get back in the ring. I miss it."

"I'm sure the other guys are glad to have you back."

"They seem to be." Nick thinks it, but doesn't say it aloud: *Although none of them can stand to look at me, as if* ugly *is contagious and they're afraid they'll carry the disease home to their loved ones if they get too close.*

The phone rings.

McDougal punches a button. "What is it, Klarissa?"

"Your wife's on line one, sir," the receptionist's voice chirps over the speakerphone. "She says it's impor—"

"Tell her to call back in ten." McDougal hangs up. "Sorry about that. I've told the silly bimbo a thousand times not to interrupt when I'm meeting with the talent. What can you do?"

Nick offers no suggestion. Everyone in the Association knows McDougal has been cheating on his wife with his receptionist for the last few years. Apparently Klarissa's skills in the bedroom (rumors abound that the boss harbors an affinity for diaper play, but you can't believe everything you hear) make up for her intellectual shortcomings.

"Nick," McDougal says, "I know you're a fellow who prefers no bullshit, so I'll cut to the chase. Due to recent...developments...we've decided to rethink your role in the GWA. I've been talking with Creative while you were recuperating, and we agreed that it might be best to drop your current character altogether."

"No more Widowmaker?" Nick's already crooked features twist into something resembling a stunned expression. He had known a fresh push would be necessary once he was back to a hundred percent. Audiences are fickle, after all. But he didn't see this coming.

"No more Widowmaker." The boss rests his elbows on his desk, steeples his fingers together. "And no more Nick Bullman."

"Let me get this straight. I flew all this way to find out you're firing me?"

"Not so fast, big fella." McDougal rises now, stands in front of the huge bay window that looks out over Wilmington, North Carolina, his hands clasped behind his back like a spoiled prince admiring his kingdom. "We've created a brand *new* character for you, actually. I think it's brilliant. Of course, I came up with it, so I admit I am a tad biased. The writing team has already begun brainstorming ideas for your first angle..."

"I'm all ears," says Nick.

"Your name will be...REVOLTO!" As he presents his idea for Nick's new character, McDougal's voice deepens, becomes gruffer as if he's narrating a bad horror movie: "No one knows where the beast comes from. Perhaps he's not even human! Some have speculated that he was sent up from the bowels of Hell by Lucifer himself to terrorize mankind. He communicates in brainless grunts and growls. He is the most dreadful animal known to man, the epitome of ugly! I mean, this friggin' guy makes the Elephant Man look like Brad Pitt. Known alternately as the Wretched One, the Most Repulsive Creature In Existence, Revolto strikes terror in the hearts of all who dare lay eyes upon his sorry excuse for a face..."

The boss sits again when he's done. Leans back in his chair. His expression hints that he might have discovered a cure for cancer, or devised a plan to eliminate world hunger. His Rolex glistens in the afternoon sunlight shining through the window behind him.

Nick glares at the C.E.O., speechless.

"Revolto will make his television debut in a hardcore brawl versus... the Widowmaker."

Nick runs a hand over his graying buzzcut, where he once sported long raven locks. He still says nothing.

"How is this possible, I know you're dying to ask? You'll be working with someone disguised as your old character. Another wrestler the same size and build as you. The Redneck Gladiator should be perfect, don't you think? We'll throw a wig on John, give him your leather duster and the face-paint. Two minutes into the Main Event, you will interfere with this fake 'Maker's match. His opponent will flee for his life. And you will *obliterate* your stand-in. There will be blood. The hard way, if necessary. That's right, Nick, I'm giving you permission to work stiff, to *shoot* if that's what it takes. I want the fans to feel every brutal, bone-shattering second of this beatdown. I want that goddamn ring to look like the floor of a *slaughterhouse* once the smoke has cleared. We'll haul 'the Widowmaker' out in a hearse at the end of the show, never to return.

"Right off the bat I'm thinking a feud with Man-Pretty is inevitable. That storyline will write itself, don't you think—the whole beauty-versus-beast, gorgeous-meets-grotesque dichotomy? Before long, Revolto will replace the Son of Eternal Darkness as the Association's most hated monster heel. And by early next year I aim to put you back on top, as our reigning Heavyweight Champ."

When he's done, McDougal's wide white grin grows wider than ever, if such a thing is possible.

"Well? What do you think?"

"You can't be serious," says Nick.

McDougal blinks. "I'm not a man who cracks jokes, Nick. You know that. What those men did to you, it's unfortunate. Personally, I hope they burn in the hottest part of Hell for it. But it happened. So we're forced to *improvise*."

When Nick doesn't respond right away, the boss says, "Let me put it this way: the marks might be easy to fool most of the time, but they aren't stupid. The last time they saw the Widowmaker, his head didn't look like six-week-old roadkill."

Nick's blood boils in his veins.

"You wanna get back on TV, surely you didn't think a mask would suffice. Latino Thugg has dibs on that gimmick. And give me one good reason why I would *want* to cover up that face! You are a promoter's wet dream, Nick. What happened to you, it is a blessing in disguise—"

"A blessing in disguise."

"You'll see."

"You've lost your fucking mind."

"I beg your pardon?"

"You think I'd allow you to exploit me like that, you've got another thing coming."

The boss's smile disappears. In its place is the glare of a man whose decisions are never disputed.

Nick stands.

"Sit down," McDougal commands.

"Not gonna happen."

"You're under contract with the Association for the next six years. You will do whatever I tell you to do."

"I'm not your carnival freak."

"Is this about *dignity*?" McDougal's cruel laughter is like a sword jabbed into the wrestler's heart. "Get that out of your head, man. Any dignity you ever had died the day your face was carved into something that looks like a bowl of mashed potatoes."

"You piece of shit," Nick growls.

"I'm sure you're harboring a lot of anger over what happened to you. But don't forget who you're talking to."

Sweat drips down the gnarled roadmap of Nick's scarred forehead, burns in his eyes.

He leaps over the C.E.O.'s desk.

Lance K. McDougal III screams.

Nick's hands wrap around the little man's neck. He doesn't let go until three Security guards burst into the office and start touching him with their Tasers.

Even then, it takes a while.

†

After the trials were over, the man formerly known as the Widowmaker moved back to Memphis, where he had bought his first home in the early days of his career. Of course, the best he could do these days was a cramped apartment on the Bad Side of Town. When all was said and done, his attorney had suggested he plant himself as far from that godforsaken business as possible. Nick concurred. It wasn't as if the smaller federations were lining up to sign him following his highly-publicized assault on the GWA's C.E.O.

Once upon a time, Nick Bullman had been a celebrity. While he was far from a household name, the die-hard fans recognized him on the street now and then. His face appeared regularly on the cover of trade magazines like *Ringside* and *Body Slam*. He drove a Hummer, had dated a few high-class strippers and even a porn star or two during his thirty-plus years in the Biz (one of the smut queens had been his third wife, in fact, though that arrangement barely lasted a month so it didn't really count). Before his life went spiraling down the shitter, he had been in talks with his agent and a ghostwriter about a possible autobiography.

But then he dared to lay his hands on Lance K. McDougal III.

When he got to thinking about it all, Nick didn't know whether to sink into a bottomless funk or never stop laughing. He had spent the last fifteen months of his life inside a courtroom. Before that he had suffered through multiple surgeries, painstaking facial reconstruction which had been only marginally successful (and calling it that was a stretch—Nick compared it to washing an old suit and smoothing out all the wrinkles, after that suit had been set on fire then buried for a year). Meanwhile, the men responsible for his condition now resided in a cushy sanitarium, where the worst thing about their lives was an eight o'clock curfew and losing games of checkers to their fellow drooling schizos.

In the case of *The State of North Carolina vs. Nicholas James Bullman*, Nick pled guilty to one count of aggravated assault. His sentence: thousands of dollars in fines, and two years' suspended probation. The judge who presided over the case—an old pal of Lance McDougal's daddy, it was rumored—informed Nick that he had considered tacking on some community service as well, perhaps a PSA appearance since the defendant was a celebrity. Alas, he had decided against it because the days of anyone wanting to see Nick Bullman's mug on TV were dead and gone. Didn't want viewers losing their dinner during prime time.

As for the civil suit that followed, McDougal's legal team demanded no less than one-point-five million dollars for what Nick had done to the C.E.O. The assault had resulted in little more than a stab to McDougal's king-sized pride, maybe a bruised windpipe and a few papercuts when Nick pulled him across the desk, but that wasn't the point. Nor was it about the money.

McDougal had sued Nick to prove that *no one* fucked with Lance K. McDougal III.

And he won.

Nick often found himself wishing he had killed the dickhead that day. If he had applied just a *few more ounces* of pressure to McDougal's pencil neck, or pitched the prick out of his twelfth-story office window...

Prison might have been preferable to living in this shithole, with only the roaches to keep him company and nothing to fill his belly but Ramen noodles and Jim Beam.

†

Sometimes, before society insisted on reminding him of the inescapable truth, he could *almost* forget about his disfigurement. For a minute or two. He certainly didn't *feel* any different. On the inside he was the same Nick Bullman he had always been, save for a newfound mistrust in his fellow man and a meek disposition that belied his muscular physique (it tends to shred a guy's self-confidence over time, venturing into public with a face once considered ruggedly handsome now reduced to a mess that would make Frankenstein's Monster piss his pants).

He could *almost* pretend he was normal. That he looked like everyone else...until he dared to leave his apartment to embark upon the necessities of middle-class life.

Take this morning. Nick had stepped out around six, traveling across town in his '93 Bronco with the terminally ill transmission, as the first rays of sunlight peeked above the horizon. His destination: the 24-Hour Grocery Outlet. He needed to pick up some toilet paper, a box of Corn Flakes and some milk, maybe a six-pack of Michelob if he had a few bucks left over. Nick always planned such trips for early in the morning or late at night. It reduced the gawking, he had learned from experience. The regulars, he could handle: the bored stares of a few red-eyed stock boys stinking of sweat and marijuana, the sad-faced single mothers working the cash registers with hickeys on their necks and tattoos like JUSTIN'S GIRL barely concealed beneath their sleeves. Some of these folks he even knew by name. They weren't the *same* employees every time, but they might as well have been. Nick assumed the graveyard crew had seen stranger sights than him lurching through their store. Maybe.

When he first spotted the kid this morning, his instincts had warned him: *Ignore it.* No good could come of striking up a conversation. He had never liked children anyway. Doubtful he would have noticed this one if not for the boy's loud sniffling; any time he went out these days, Nick wore sunglasses and a hooded sweatshirt, which helped hide his face from the rest of the world but it killed his peripheral vision.

The kid was four or five years old. He wore an Incredible Hulk T-shirt that was stained all over with something matching the color of his favorite hero's flesh.

"Where's my mommy?" he sobbed.

Nick approached the child against his better judgment. "Hey there. You lost? It's okay, son. We'll find your mama."

The instant the brat saw what lurked within that colossal reaper's cowl, he started screeching at the top of his lungs.

It was the most nerve-wracking sound the big man had ever heard. It made his *teeth* hurt.

"Aww, shit."

"*Mommy!* Somebody help me! It's...a *monster!*"

A moment later, the misplaced mommy in question stumbled around the corner, her trailer-park high heels clicking out a white-trash rhythm on the store's recently polished floor.

When she saw Nick standing over her son, her mouth stretched into a wide black "O." She slapped at his chest with her massive pink pocketbook, demanding to know what he was doing to her beloved Billy Junior. Was he some kinda kiddie-lovin' pervert? He sure looked like a weirdo, weren't no doubt about that.

"Somebody call nine-one-one!" her voice echoed through the store. "I think he tried to touch my boy!"

Nick didn't wait around to hear more.

He ran. Collided with a Cheez-Its display. Boxes flew everywhere, an avalanche of red and orange. In retrospect, he supposed his clumsy getaway made him appear guilty of *something*, but his only concern had been getting the hell out of there.

To top off everything else, once he reached his Bronco in the parking lot she teased him for a minute before starting ("Come on, you twat," Nick growled, "don't do this to me"). Took him four tries before she caught.

Nope, it certainly had *not* been his favorite morning ever.

†

The second he walked through the door of his apartment following his ill-fated trip to the grocery store, his phone rang.

He almost didn't answer it. But he welcomed this opportunity to take out his anger on an early-bird telemarketer or some asswipe with a wrong number.

The *last* thing Nick expected to hear was that single word on the other end of the line: "...Daddy?"

†

He fell into his recliner. Fell into it hard. Swallowed a fist-sized lump in his throat. It went down, but got stuck somewhere around his heart.

Six years had passed since the last time he'd heard that voice. It had been nearly twice as long since he'd seen her in person.

"Melissa?"

She was his only child. Well, the only one he knew about. In that respect, his life on the road had been similar to a rock star's. He remembered the ring rats scurrying backstage after every show, practically biting and clawing at one another for a chance to meet him. Even following the birth of his reviled Widowmaker character—when he had ditched his do-gooder babyface role once and for all—there had been no shortage of sluts. Sometimes he asked for their names when it was over. Usually he didn't. He'd never given a damn anyway.

Melissa's mother, though...she'd been different.

Before the fame, before the hangers-on and the skanks throwing themselves at his feet, Arlene had truly *loved* him.

Once upon a time, they shared something special.

They'd been high school sweethearts. But what really made Nick fall for her was her selfless dedication toward helping him pursue *his* goals. She never scoffed at his dream of becoming a professional wrestler, had stood by him as he paid his proverbial dues first as a student of Big Jim Brogan's Five-Star Wrestling School in Midnight, North Carolina, then when he was hired on as a bottom-tier rookie in the Global Wrestling Association several years later. She never left his side, figuratively at least, even after their relationship became a long-distance affair, when he traveled from coast to coast working the dark matches. Though the lovebirds wished they could be together twenty-four seven, Nick barely made enough dough to feed himself back then. He had sworn to her that one day their sacrifices *would* pay off. And when that day finally came, he vowed to treat her like a queen.

Then Arlene got pregnant.

He found out about it ten minutes before his first televised match, when his stomach was already doing somersaults and he'd been sure he was gonna puke his guts out.

Almost immediately, upon receiving the news, Nick began to distance himself from this young lady he once thought he loved more than anything else in the world.

The moment she informed him that he was going to be a father, things *changed*.

He wasn't proud of it. But that was who he had been back then. The Nick Bullman of three decades ago—the hungry kid who had worked so hard to prove to his superiors and the fans that he would one day be the best in the Biz—hadn't been willing to slam on the brakes so abruptly. He refused to put his dreams on hold in order to accept this new responsibility.

He wasn't ready to be a father. A husband. A nobody. He was ready to be a *star*.

He had tried to rationalize his behavior. Tried to convince himself, even as he failed to show up again and again when he promised to visit Arlene and little Melissa, that he was doing the right thing. Giving fatherhood his best shot, while keeping his eyes on the Big Picture.

Hard to be a devoted family man, though, when you're in Hawaii one week, Tokyo the next. Meanwhile, said family sits in their drafty mobile home in the mountains of North Carolina, waiting for your call.

The years sped by, and while Nick never vanished completely from his daughter's life, the occasions when he did make time for her grew further and further apart. Eventually, Arlene moved on. She told him she could no longer commit herself to a man who might as well have been a ghost, a man who had severed ties with those who loved him because the only person in the world he ever truly cared about was *himself.*

In what felt like the blink of an eye, Nick Bullman's little girl was no longer a little girl at all.

The last time he had seen his daughter she was nineteen years old. Now her thirtieth birthday was just a few months away. If he remembered correctly.

His regret was like some parasitic worm coiled inside of him. It had been dormant for a while, but now it awoke to feed again.

A sniffle on the other end of the line brought him back to the present: "Daddy? Are you there?"

"I'm here," Nick replied.

His voice was a pitiful croak. He cleared his throat, said it again. "Yeah, baby...I'm here."

✝

"Daddy, I need you."

"Melissa..."

Her voice grew thick, wet, nearly unintelligible, and beneath her tears she was obviously talking more to herself than to him at first: "Don't know what the hell I was thinking...oughta have my head examined for getting mixed up with him in the first place..."

"Melissa, what's going on? Did somebody hurt you?"

"I wish you could drive out here. I wish you could come right now. It's a lot to ask, I know, but...do you think you could?" She sounded lost, alone, more like a terrified child than a woman on the brink of turning thirty. "I didn't know who else to call. *Please*, Daddy..."

Her whole life, he'd been Missing In Action. Nick Bullman didn't know his daughter's favorite food, what she did for a living, or her most cherished childhood memory. They were barely more than strangers. But she was his blood.

"Can you come? Please?" she asked him again.

Her sobs wrenched at his heart.

Nick took a long look around his apartment: at the bile-colored sofa with its foam guts leaking out...at the wide brown water stain on the ceiling that grew bigger every day...at the two fat bluebottle flies fucking on a dust-covered windowsill. He sighed, knew he could turn his back on all of it. His boss would probably raise hell if he asked for a few days off. Then again, Nick wasn't entirely sure if he still had his gig at the Cherry Pit (two days ago a regular had complained to management about how he came to spend his dough on pretty girls but it was "hard to get in the mood with a bouncer standing nearby whose face looked like a plate of raw hamburger").

After McDougal's lawsuit wiped him out, Nick could no longer lay claim to a hefty nest egg sitting in the bank. Nothing substantial, anyway. But he supposed he could afford to leave town for a little while. Assuming his piece-of-shit Bronco didn't break down somewhere on the side of I-40.

In less than a minute, his decision was made. His daughter needed him. For once, by God, he would be there for her.

"Where are you, hon? Do you still live in Midnight?"

"I do," she said. "I know it's a lot to ask, but—"

"Where should we meet? Got a nine-hour drive ahead of me. I leave now, I can be there before dark."

†

He pulled into Midnight, North Carolina around five-thirty that evening. He didn't know how long he would be needed here, so he had packed enough clothes to last him a week. The old gym bag sat beside him on the Bronco's passenger seat like his only friend in the world. On the truck's CD player, Howlin' Wolf insisted he was built for comfort, not for speed.

Moments after Nick passed the sign welcoming him to Midnight (he noticed the subscript that once boasted BIRTHPLACE OF TV WRESTLER NICK BULLMAN! was gone now, presumably since around the time his own face was erased), he found himself overwhelmed by how much everything had changed. At the corner of First and Main, the old Midnight Drug & Sundry had been replaced by a massive bank with fancy mirrored windows. A block further down, where Hank's Hobby Shop and Corriher Guns n' Ammo once sat side by side, he saw a Jiffy Lube, a Domino's Pizza, and a Chinese take-out joint. The Big Pig Grocery had become a sprawling used-car lot. Old Man Dickerson's newsstand, where young Nick Bullman used to buy his beloved Superman comic books, was now a Radio Shack. Though it didn't surprise him at all to see that the Lansdale Drive-In Theater was gone, he couldn't help but feel a sharp pang of disappointment when he passed the Wal-Mart in its place.

Nick shook his head as he took it all in, his lipless mouth pinching together into something resembling a sad smile.

When he at last reached his destination, he took a deep breath, let it out slowly. On the phone, his daughter had asked him if he remembered where he had taken her for dinner on her thirteenth birthday (she didn't remind him that this was the last time he had acknowledged her birthday at all, but she didn't have to). He did recall the place, and he had agreed to meet her at that address. He expected to see a Subway or a Burger King sitting there at the south end of Main Street. He couldn't believe Annie's Country Diner was still around.

He parked in front of the restaurant, between a gray utility van and a mud-spattered pickup with a gun rack in the rear window.

He turned off the Bronco's ignition. Realized his hands were shaking as he pulled his handkerchief from his back pocket and dabbed at his leaking right eye.

For several minutes he just sat there, wondering what the hell he was going to say to his daughter after so many years.

Finally, he pulled his hood over his head, and climbed out of the vehicle.

†

The place smelled like fried chicken and coffee. *Not* two of Nick's favorite smells: when he was a kid, his father used to task him with beheading the birds on their farm, and ever since then the aroma of frying chicken made him sick to his stomach; likewise, he had never developed a taste for java, unlike just about everyone else he had ever known.

There were a dozen or so customers in the diner. At least half of them turned to stare as he entered. Conversations halted, and for several seconds the only sounds were the grill sizzling in the kitchen and a cook's voice calling out from back there: "Chuckwagon plate's up, Brenda!" The people who had stopped eating to gawk at Nick did not return to their meals right away. A young mother pinched her son's forearm, admonishing him about how it wasn't polite to stare. At the bar beside the cash register, a dreadlocked twenty-something in a tie-dyed T-shirt mumbled "oh, that poor individual" to his chubby girlfriend, but when he swiveled back around on his stool he slid his plate of corned beef hash to one side.

A waitress passed by, and without looking in Nick's direction she said, "Seat yourself, be with ya soon as I can." She was a living, breathing cliché with her orange hairdo, her rumpled uniform, the way she smacked at her gum like a cow working at a mouthful of cud.

"No problem." Behind his dark glasses, Nick's eyes skimmed the restaurant. "I'm meeting someone."

The waitress had already moved on, and was catering to the culinary needs of three burly rednecks. She cackled loudly as one of the men said something hilarious, pulled her down onto his lap.

Nick didn't need her anyway. Because a moment later he found who he was looking for.

She sat in a corner booth. Her back was turned to him. He could not see his daughter's face. But he *knew* her. As if via some sixth sense, blood drawn to blood.

She wore a faded denim jacket with a small rip in the left shoulder. A cloud of cigarette smoke hovered over her table like a bad omen.

Slowly, Nick approached his daughter.

As he crossed the diner, he searched for something to do with his hands. They were two enormous slabs of meat that existed only to get in his way. He shoved them into the pockets of his jeans. Pulled them out. Shoved them back in.

When he at last stood over her, he cleared his throat.

She turned to face him.

Nick barely caught himself—his initial instinct was not unlike the averted-eyes reaction so many people gave *him* these days, when they saw his mangled features.

She was twenty-nine. But she looked at least ten years older than that.

Sitting before him, Nick knew, was a soul defeated. Someone to whom life had been unkind.

An icy fist squeezed his heart as she slid out of the booth and wrapped her arms around him.

"You, uh, wanna sit down?" she said when that was done.

She took her seat again, and he crammed his bulk into the opposite side of the booth.

Right away, Nick noticed that his daughter didn't seem fazed by his appearance. He found that odd. She *was* aware of what had happened to him three years ago—he had received word after the fact that she had called to check on him while he was in the hospital—but this was the first time Melissa had seen for herself the grisly results of his encounter with Rebel Yell and One-Arm. Perhaps whatever was troubling her was so awful she barely recognized the extent of her father's disfigurement. Or she simply did not care.

Why the hell should she? Nick thought.

She sat there staring at a cup of coffee in front of her as if it held the answers to all of her problems. A cigarette burned in an overflowing ashtray in the center of the table.

She wore no makeup. Faint acne scars dotted her cheeks and forehead. Her dark brown hair looked as if she had last washed it weeks ago. Nick reached across the table, gently pushed several oily strands of it out of her face.

She flinched when he touched her. But then she offered him a halfhearted smile. A smile that did not reach her eyes.

"Melissa, tell me what's going on."

She sniffled, turned to stare out the restaurant's plate-glass window. Across the street sat the white-brick building that housed the adjacent offices of the *Midnight Sun* and the Polk County Sheriff's Department. The way she looked at the latter made Nick think of a junkie gazing upon her next fix, if said fix was located on the opposite side of a bottomless rift.

His big hands reached for hers. "Talk to me, girl. I'm here."

"You'll never know how much this means to me." She continued to stare out the window, and her pale reflection gazed back like a phantom voyeur eavesdropping on their awkward reunion. "Your coming here, I mean."

"It's the least I could do," said Nick.

"I didn't want to bother you, Daddy. But I didn't know who else to call."

He shifted in his seat, and now he stared out the window with her. He cleared his throat again. "There is, um, one thing. Before we go any further."

"What?"

"I was thinking...maybe you shouldn't call me that. You know I don't deserve it."

She took a drag off her cigarette. He noticed her fingernails were chewed down into the quick.

"After all this time, it doesn't feel right, does it?" he asked her. "I don't mind if you call me Nick. I think that might be best."

She shrugged, exhaled a wisp of smoke from one side of her mouth. Her tone was slightly defiant, or perhaps she was simply too tired to argue. "I'm a big girl. It's not a huge deal."

"Somebody who was there for you, did the things fathers are supposed to do, he deserves to be called Daddy. Not me. That fella your momma married, what's his name again?"

"Warren."

"He took care of you, when I was off acting like an asshole. You should call him Dad."

"Warren was a pervert. And he died in that car accident the year after Mom got cancer."

Nick would have winced if his ruined features allowed it. "I'm sorry."

They were both quiet for the next minute or two. Nick's heart felt heavier than ever.

The orange-haired waitress appeared before their table. "Did ya need to see a menu?" she asked Nick, although her eyes were glued to the order pad in her hand.

"Nothing for me."

"Refill your coffee?"

Nick's daughter gave a barely perceptible shake of her head. She took one last drag off her cigarette, snubbed it out.

"I'll get your check, then."

The moment they were alone again, Melissa buried her face in her hands and started sobbing.

Nick sensed the other customers watching them, but he couldn't have cared less. He removed his sunglasses, looked into his daughter's swollen red eyes. This time she allowed his giant hands to engulf her own.

"I want to help you, Melissa, but I can't do that unless you tell me what's wrong."

"Somebody took her," she cried. "They took my Sophie away, and I don't know whether she's alive or dead. For all I know she could be lying in a ditch somewhere, raped and...murdered. And it's...all my fault..."

"What are you talking about? Who is Sophie?"

Melissa blew her nose into a handful of napkins before replying, "Sophie is your granddaughter."

†

She had a story to tell. It was a long one. Where minutes ago he had begged her to open up to him, a flood of secrets gushed out of her now. Occasionally she paused to light another cigarette, or to gaze out the window again. But even when she stopped speaking for a minute or more Nick kept his questions to himself.

His mind, body, and soul felt numb as he listened to his daughter's every word...

†

She said:

"When I was a teenager, I made Mom's life a living hell. I'm not proud of it, but it's true. I used to come home late every night smelling like pot and beer. I ran with a bad crowd, guys older than me who only wanted one thing but I was too stupid to realize it.

"I guess you can see where this is going. A few weeks before my sixteenth birthday, I got knocked up. I was such a mess I didn't even know who the father was.

"I named the baby Sophie. Sophia Lynn. I wasn't mature enough to raise a child. I was just a kid myself. But after Mom and I saw her for the first time, we couldn't bring ourselves to give Sophie away to some stranger. You remember Mom's sister, Aunt Patty? We worked things out so *she* would take Sophie. That way we could see her any time we wanted.

"For the first twelve years of my daughter's life, that arrangement worked out fine...

But the summer before last, I decided to come clean with Sophie.

She always knew she was adopted—up till that point, I was 'Aunt Melissa.' The older Sophie got, though...it hurt so much, driving up to Hickory to visit her every few months, seeing how my little girl was starting to look just like me. I couldn't live a lie any longer.

"I was afraid she'd never wanna see me again when I told her the truth. But that wasn't how it turned out at all. We couldn't wait to start over, to catch up on all that mother-daughter stuff I used to worry I'd never be worth a damn at. I realized how much I had missed out on. I felt like I'd been given a chance to right all my wrongs. I didn't want to spend another second of my life without Sophie by my side.

"I think that's why I can't find it inside of myself to hate you, Dad— er, *Nick*. God knows I wanted to hate your guts, after Mom died and I felt like I didn't have anybody in the world who gave a shit about me. But I couldn't. 'Cause I had done the same thing to Sophie. I checked in on her, sure, I dropped by Aunt Patty's to see her, but it was always at my convenience.

"The first time she called me 'Mom,' when I took her back home one evening after we'd spent the weekend together, I stayed up all night crying into my pillow. I felt like some missing piece of me had finally been put into place.

"I really thought we were gonna make it, Sophie and me. I know we would have been okay, if it wasn't for this guy I'd been seeing...

"I met Eddie a couple years ago. A girl I used to work with had been trying to hook us up as long as I'd known her. I finally agreed just to shut her up. Next thing I know, I'm sitting in the bleachers at the Polk County Race Track with Deb, her old man, and Eddie at a freaking *demolition derby*. It wasn't the most romantic date I've ever been on. Should've been a sign right there. Something about Eddie, though...I don't know how to explain it. I fell for him, head over heels. I let my trailer get repo'd so I could move in with him. I quit my job at the Waffle House. He told me I didn't have to worry about anything, he'd take care of me 'cause I was his *gal*.

"Looking back, I knew Eddie was no good. I knew it, but I stayed with him anyway. I've always been like that. Ever since I reached that age when I started acting all boy-crazy, I always chased after the ones I knew were bad for me.

"When we first got together, Eddie told me he made his living doing a bunch of odd jobs around town. Painting houses, cleaning out gutters, crap like that. But I knew there had to be something else going on. His cellphone rang all hours of the night. And his wallet stayed so *fat* all the time! I always suspected it wasn't legal, whatever he was into. I guess that's why I never nagged him about it, 'cause I didn't *want* to know the truth.

"One night not long after I moved in with him, Eddie stepped out to buy a pack of cigarettes. While he was gone I heard a knock at the door. There was this strung-out-looking skank standing on our front porch. She pulled a wad of cash out of her bra, asked me to tell Eddie how sorry she was for being late with it, promised it'd never happen again.

"Of course, I confronted him about it when he got home. Turned into this huge fight. But Eddie finally came clean about everything...

"He was a drug dealer. And a pimp. Smalltime stuff, mostly. Weed, pills, crystal meth. Sherrie was one of his whores, worked the truck stops off I-26 outside of town. That's where he moved most of his crank, too—long-haul drivers call it 'high speed chicken feed,' use it to stay awake on the road.

"Even after I found out all that shit, I didn't break it off with him. I rationalized my staying with Eddie by telling myself that he was good to me. Far as I knew, he didn't screw around. Sure, he sold drugs, thought he was some kinda redneck mack-daddy with those sluts he had working for him, but he treated me right. It was like, once I got mixed up with him, I turned into that stupid teenager I used to be all over again.

"Earlier this summer, even though a little voice inside my head kept telling me it was a bad idea, I decided Sophie should come live with us. Of course, Aunt Patty was against it. We had a big falling-out the day I loaded up Sophie's stuff in Eddie's truck. She said I had never been responsible before, so what made me think I could start now. She begged Sophie not to go. Even threatened to take me to court, but nothing ever came of that.

"I don't know what the hell I was thinking. I guess I hoped...I might be able to *change* Eddie. If I could get him to make an honest living, maybe we could be a happy family. I know it was stupid. But Sophie seemed to like Eddie a lot, and although a guy like Eddie could never be the 'father figure' type, he thought she was okay too. A few weeks before... what happened...he took her out for her birthday, got her a tattoo. Shoulda been illegal considering she's a minor, but Eddie knew people. He always *knew people*. It was this tiny thing, a yin-yang symbol on her ankle, but we fought about that for days. Of course, any time I tried to talk to him about the other stuff, about the dealing and the pimping, he accused me of nagging. He asked me why couldn't I be happy, when he took care of me and Sophie and we didn't have to worry about a thing. He'd ball up his fists like he wanted to hit me. He never did lay a hand on me. But when we argued...Eddie always looked like he was so full of anger it was bubbling up inside of him just waiting to blow. Sometimes he reminded me of this frightened little boy, constantly looking over his shoulder like a monster was gonna come gobble him up.

"I guess whatever he was afraid of, whatever filled Eddie with that rage...it finally caught up with him.

"After Sophie moved in with us, I decided to go back to work. I didn't want to rely on Eddie's dirty money anymore. I got a job waiting tables at a bar just over the county line. It wasn't the classiest job ever, didn't bring in half the dough Eddie was carrying home night after night, but ya know what? At least I could look my daughter in the face and give her an honest answer when she asked me what *I* did for a living. In the meantime, I kept praying that I'd be a good influence on Eddie. That he would want to do the right thing, for Sophie and me. But he never got the chance...

"It happened three weeks ago. Another girl had called in sick and I was the only one working the floor that night. I didn't get home till two in the morning.

"I knew something was wrong as soon as I pulled into the driveway. Eddie's pickup was there, but it had jumped the curb. It was parked half in our yard, half in the road. Its driver-side door was hanging open. The front door of our house was wide open, too.

"The first thing I noticed when I stepped inside the house was the smell of blood. It was so strong I could *taste* it.

"I found Eddie in the hallway. Somebody had...blown his head off. With a shotgun. He was lying on his stomach and his...brains...were splashed all over the carpet.

"I ran to Sophie's room, screaming her name. But she was gone. There weren't any signs of a struggle. Her bedroom looked just like it always did, except some of her clothes were missing. Her closet door was open. Her dresser drawers had been pulled out. Like she'd packed her stuff in a hurry.

"We were getting along so well, finally building a life together. I never should've insisted that she come live with us. Aunt Patty was right. She was happy up there. Safe. Now I don't know whether my daughter is alive or dead. And it's all my fault.

"Oh, God, it's all *my fault...*"

†

When she was done Melissa sank even further into her seat, and from the back of her throat came a moan of despair. Her hands splayed out before her on the tabletop, as if she feared she might fall off of this world if she didn't hold on to something.

"I'll be damned," said Nick. "I'm a *grandfather?*"

"It's true."

"I can't believe your mother never told me."

"*No one* knew. We had the arrangement with Aunt Patty. By the time I got pregnant, you were barely calling more than once or twice a year. Mom thought it wouldn't matter one way or the other if you did know."

Nick had never felt so low.

"I didn't say that to hurt you," she assured him.

"No. If the shoe fits, right?"

In her distressed features Nick could see the little girl his daughter had once been. A child he had barely known, but whom he recognized, however vaguely.

He shifted in his seat, decided there would be time for apologies later. "What are the police saying about this? There must have been some kind of search party?"

Melissa picked up her battered pack of cigarettes, but then realized she had already smoked her last one. She cursed under her breath, let the empty pack drop back onto the tabletop.

"They made a big show of it at first," she said. "A bunch of guys from the Rescue Squad dragged the river. That was the hardest thing I ever had to watch. Sheriff Mackey keeps telling me he hasn't given up, but then in the same breath he says most missing teenagers are missing because they *want* to be. Thing is, to the cops Eddie was just a piece-of-shit drug dealer. They're not in any hurry to arrest whoever killed him."

"Wait," said Nick. "You don't mean—"

"They think Eddie...touched her. That maybe he'd been doing it for a while, and she finally had enough."

Nick swallowed a sick taste in his mouth. "Melissa, forgive me. Could they be on to something?"

"No way. Eddie wasn't a good guy, I know that. But he never

would've laid a hand on Sophie."

Nick nodded, though he refused to rule anything out for now. "She's a suspect, then?"

"Not officially. But they keep calling her a 'person of interest.' Whatever that means. They even questioned Aunt Patty at one point. They thought *she* might be hiding Sophie away. Of course, we're not on speaking terms anymore. Aunt Patty blames me for everything."

"What do *you* think happened that night?" Nick asked her.

"I think Sophie witnessed Eddie's murder. And whoever killed him kidnapped her 'cause she'd seen too much."

"What about his truck? You said it was sitting up on the curb when you got home, with the door open. Sounds to me like he might have been running from somebody."

"That's what I thought. Still do. But according to Sheriff Mackey, the autopsy showed Eddie's blood-alcohol level was over twice the legal limit. Their theory is, he came home shitfaced, went after Sophie but she was waiting for him."

Nick took a minute or two to let everything she had told him sink in.

"Any way you look at it, it doesn't make a damn bit of sense," he said. "She takes the time to go through her closet, pack a change of clothes, after she's just witnessed your boyfriend's murder? I don't buy it. She would have been scared to death. She would have gotten out of that house as soon as possible. Hid in the woods till the killer took off, I don't know. But she wouldn't just hang around. Which means one of two things: either the cops are right, and she killed Eddie—you do need to prepare yourself for that possibility, Melissa—or his murderer allowed her to take some of her things along for a reason."

"Oh, God."

"Whoever killed Eddie, he didn't want any witnesses, he wouldn't have hesitated to kill her too. But if we're onto something here, this person made her pack a change of clothes. That means your daughter is *alive*. And he planned to keep her that way."

"But what did he want with her? What is he doing to my baby *right now*?" Melissa sobbed.

Nick shook his head, didn't know how to answer that. He opted not to mention another possibility: that his granddaughter might have been in cahoots with the culprit even if she didn't pull the trigger.

"She took her medicine with her too," Melissa said. "Every time I think about that I want to break down again."

"Medicine?"

"Lamictal. Sophie's epileptic. It keeps her from having seizures."

Nick's heart ached worse than ever for this young lady—both of them—who shared his blood yet remained a mystery to him.

"She refused to go anywhere without her pills. Back when we were still talking, Aunt Patty told me Sophie had a seizure at school one time. Ever since, she's been mortified at the thought of it happening again in public. She said a bunch of stuck-up cheerleader types recorded the whole thing on their iPhones so they could all laugh at it later."

"How often does she have to take this—"

"Lamictal. Twice a day, every day."

Melissa started sobbing again.

Around them, the sounds of the restaurant seemed a million miles away now: silverware clinking against dishes...the gurgle of a coffeemaker... the *thwap* of a spatula slapping meat patties on the grill.

Nick sighed, rubbed at the stubble beneath his misshapen chin. His five o'clock shadow started low, halfway down his neck, as his disfigured face was completely hairless, like a plot of scorched earth where not even a single weed could survive.

"I'm assuming I'm here 'cause you want to me to try to find her," he said. "You think there's something I can do that the law can't?"

"I was hoping you could talk to some people who might not give the police the time of day," Melissa said. "If the cops don't intimidate them... maybe you can."

"Maybe," said Nick.

"It's been three weeks since Sophie disappeared. The cops are clueless. But I know she's alive. I can feel it. She's just waiting for us to come save her."

"Melissa..."

"Will you try? Please? That's all I'm asking. Will you *try* to find my baby?"

Nick took a deep breath, let it out slowly.

"Please," she said again.

"I'll do what I can."

Even as the words fell from his mouth he had no idea what they meant. And he feared he might regret them.

"You need to understand, though: I'm not the police. I'm not some private dick. These days I'm just a bouncer with a bum knee and a fucked-up face. Used to be a grappler, so I had a few moves once upon a time. I doubt I've got those anymore. The last thing I wanna do is get your hopes up, sweetheart. Promise me you won't get your hopes up."

"I won't," she said.

"Sounds like your boyfriend was mixed up in some bad business. I might look like something out of a horror flick, but I go pushing my weight around, trying to get answers from people who don't wanna give them, somebody else could get hurt."

"I understand."

"Good. Tell me how to get to Eddie's place."

"You remember the old train depot just outside of Midnight?"

Nick remembered it well. Once, after a fight with his father when he was twelve, he had decided to run away from home. Packing a bag lunch and his life's savings at the time (five dollars), he had set out to ride the nation's rails like a hobo, embarking on nomadic adventures with no parents telling him what he could and couldn't do. He got as far as the Polk County Train Depot before he chickened out, hightailing it back home into the arms of his distraught mother.

Melissa said, "Just past the depot, you'll see Gorman Gap Road on your right. After about a mile you'll pass an old church. There's a cow pasture, then Eddie's is the first house on the left. His name's on the mailbox: Whiteside. You can't miss it. There's still police tape everywhere."

"Got it."

Nick slid out of the booth. He could feel everyone in the restaurant staring at him as he stood. Once again, he ignored them.

"You're going out there right now?" Melissa asked him.

"Can't think of a better place to start."

✝

Since the night Sophie disappeared, Melissa had been renting an apartment on the edge of town. She insisted Nick come stay with her, but he didn't feel comfortable with the thought of moving in even temporarily with his adult daughter, the fact that they were practically strangers notwithstanding. After leaving Annie's Country Diner, he drove to the Sunrise Motor Lodge off North Main, where he rented a room for a week. It wasn't the fanciest joint in the world, but it would do in a bind.

Melissa gave him her phone number, a key to the house she had shared with Eddie, and a wallet-sized photo of her daughter.

She begged him to be careful. He promised her he could take care of himself.

As they left the diner, Nick noticed the flyers up and down the block: stapled to telephone poles, taped to storefronts. He hadn't paid them any attention on his way into town but now they were impossible to miss. HAVE YOU SEEN ME? read the caption at the top, above a black-and-white reproduction of the photo Melissa had given him. Beneath that: SOPHIE LYNN SUTTLES/AGE 14/MISSING SINCE JUNE 26, followed by a contact number for the Polk County Sheriff's Department.

Nick and his daughter embraced as the patrons of Annie's Country Diner watched through the restaurant's windows. Overhead, out front of the Sheriff's Department, the U.S. and North Carolina-state flags flapped and clanked against their pole like the voice of the town itself warning Nick that he could do no good here.

Just before he climbed into his Bronco, and she into her green Camry parked on the opposite side of the street, Nick looked back to see Melissa glaring at their audience. If she'd been packing, he was quite sure she would have opened fire on every last one of them.

"Oh, take a fucking picture," she said.

He told her, "Hang around me long enough, hon, you're gonna have to get used to that."

✝

Nick popped his favorite album, a collection of old blues tunes, into the Bronco's CD player. The hairs on the nape of his neck stood up as Lightnin' Hopkins sang of going back home: *"Well, you know this ain't no place for me, and I don't think po' Lightnin' wanna stay..."*

As he drove out of Midnight's town proper and into the countryside bordering Polk County, Nick passed a few of his old haunts, and he wondered what had become of others: places like Storch's Rim, where he had lost his virginity at the age of fifteen...the graffiti bridge near Junction 108, beneath which he had sipped his first beer and toked on his first joint...that secret spot in the Snake River Woods where he used to throw pennies into an old well, wishing he could one day be rich and famous just like his idol, Elvis. He nearly grew dizzy beneath the memories.

He followed Melissa's directions without consciously thinking about them. His formative years had been spent here, and in many ways it felt as if he had left Midnight only yesterday. Before long, a crooked old one-room church zipped by in his peripheral vision, then a sprawling green pasture in which eight or nine fat black cows grazed behind a barbed-wire fence.

Nick maneuvered the Bronco around a deep curve, and his destination was upon him.

He turned down the music.

The house was small, beige with brown trim. Its gravel driveway was littered with the glistening green fragments of a broken beer bottle. A propane grill leaned against one side of the house. Ribbons of yellow crime-scene tape crisscrossed the front porch ("NO TRESPASSING BY ORDER OF POLK COUNTY SHERIFF'S DEPT"). At some point a strip of it had come loose; it dangled from the spidery branches of a dead rosebush in the middle of the yard, snapping and popping in the afternoon breeze. A thick copse of trees lined the rear of the property like a crowd of curious bystanders hoping to catch a glimpse of something gruesome.

Nick stared down at the photo of his granddaughter that Melissa had given him. Before pulling out of his parking space back at the diner, he had placed the picture on his dashboard next to the Bronco's speedometer.

The teenager's eyes were a radiant blue. Like his own. Her round face showed a hint of the chubby child she must have been at one time. Her dark brown hair was trimmed in a pageboy style. She wore a maroon leather jacket over a gray T-shirt, a Celtic cross necklace. The corners of her mouth were turned up in a mischievous grin, as if Sophie knew a secret that could tear this town apart.

Nick wondered what she was like. If she was safe. If he would soon be blessed with the opportunity to get to know his granddaughter, or if it was already too late.

A horn honked.

He glanced in the Bronco's cracked rearview mirror, saw a sour-faced man in a dusty VW bug behind him.

He threw up one hand, quickly pulled over to the shoulder.

The man tooted his horn again. As the Beetle puttered on down the road, Nick noticed a faded bumper sticker on its back window: JESUS IS COMING, R U READY? He wondered if it was *that* appointment the guy had been so afraid he'd miss.

He killed the Bronco's ignition.

Wondered why he was here.

What the hell did he plan to do now? What was he looking for, exactly? He didn't have a clue. But he had promised Melissa he would try.

He leaned over, scrounged around in the glove compartment until he found an old pair of work gloves. They had been crammed down in there ever since he first bought the Bronco secondhand, and he had never gotten around to throwing them out. He slid them into his back pocket, just in case (he was about to go snooping around a *crime scene*, after all).

He climbed out of the Bronco. Pulled back his hood. His shaved scalp and gnarled forehead were slick with sweat.

He crossed the road and stepped onto the overgrown lawn. The high grass whispered against his shins. It had rained here recently; the air smelled of mud and, faintly, manure from the pasture down the road.

Nick took the three steps leading up to the porch in a single stride, ducking through a gap in the police tape to access the front door.

He dug into his pocket for the key Melissa had given him.

But then his breath caught in his throat.

At one time, more of that yellow crime-scene tape had been stretched across the threshold to warn away the curious. Now it lay in a pile at Nick's feet, like a dead snake.

The door was ajar. The lock had been busted.

Nick gently pushed on the door, forcing it open just far enough so he could enter by turning sideways. He wondered if he should announce his presence, call out to whomever might still be in the house. No...he decided it would be best to keep the element of surprise in his favor till he knew what he was up against.

He stepped through a small living room, past a recliner, a loveseat, and a coffee table stained with old cup-rings. The house was dark. It had that stale "closed-in" odor of a place that has been empty of any human presence for a while, a smell that was not too strong but still slightly unpleasant. Against one wall stood a widescreen TV and a tall potted plant that had starved to death weeks ago.

In the hallway that connected the living room to the rear of the house, the beige carpet was matted with an ugly maroon blotch. The stain spread out approximately three feet in diameter, but did not stop at the baseboard; it climbed several inches up the wall in a starburst pattern. Dozens of black dots speckled the wall as well—damage left by the spray of shotgun pellets.

It didn't take a genius to figure out that this was the spot where Eddie had been murdered.

Nick swallowed a foul taste in his mouth, stepped over the stain.

...and he heard a loud *THUMP* toward the back of the house.

He froze.

Another *THUD*, followed by a muffled curse.

He wished he had a weapon. Thought about going back for the tire iron in his truck. Tried not to think about the possibility that he might be creeping up on a trigger-happy cop.

He took another cautious step forward.

He had never realized how difficult it was for a guy his size to *sneak*. Of course, with the exception of a crude storyline in the early days of his "feud" with Big Bubba Bad-Ass—he had "broken into" Eric's house, and as the marks booed him on the Widowmaker "planted video cameras" throughout his enemy's home: in a bedroom, the shower, everywhere Big Bubba shared intimate moments with his bikini-model wife—Nick Bullman had never had any *reason* to sneak around. He feared that his every step could be heard all the way back in Midnight. He imagined the customers in Annie's Country Diner holding on to their seats, staring wide-eyed at the ripples in their coffee each time one of his Size 16 boots touched the floor.

He sucked in a deep breath, held it as he moved through the house: past a cluttered utility room...a bathroom so tiny he suspected he'd get stuck if he tried to turn around in there...and a bedroom decorated with posters of brooding, black-clad rock stars. The latter, he assumed, was where his granddaughter once slept.

Again he heard movement. It came from the master bedroom up ahead, on his right. Sounded like someone searching for something—drawers being yanked open, footsteps pacing back and forth. And, every few seconds, exasperated curses in a thick Southern accent...

"Dammit, you gotta be in here somewhere!"

Nick slid along the wall, inching closer, until he stood just three or four feet from the open doorway of the master bedroom.

A floorboard creaked beneath his boot.

The noises abruptly ceased.

Nick mouthed a breathless curse. He stood statue-still. Waiting, listening. Wishing again that he had a weapon...

After for what felt like forever, he again moved toward the bedroom.

He risked a glance through the doorway.

Clothes were tangled and strewn all over the floor. On the king-sized bed lay jagged pieces of a shattered acoustic guitar. A lamp dangled off a nightstand, its cord stretched taut. Against the wall to Nick's right stood a large mirrored dresser; half of its drawers hung open, the other half were dumped upside-down on the floor.

Nick stepped into the bedroom.

He was alone. But how...?

At the back of the room a thin doorway opened onto another small bathroom. A rectangle of evening sunlight bled through a frosted-glass window above the toilet. He wondered if whomever had been making all that racket had escaped through that window. Impossible. It appeared to be merely decorative, and was just slightly wider than a cereal box.

Which meant that the intruder had to *still be in this room*—

A *slosh*ing noise behind him. In the mirror above the dresser: a glimpse of wild, bloodshot eyes. A *man*, moving fast. Something big and box-shaped (and filled with *water*?) hefted above his head.

Nick turned. Too late.

The CRASH was louder than anything he had ever heard. Felt like a damn *planet* dropped on top of his skull, as his senses were assaulted by an explosion of wet, stink, and pain.

He fell to one knee beneath a shower of broken glass and foul-smelling water.

"Aww, shit!" said a voice that seemed to come from a million miles away at first. "Not *you*! What have I *done*?"

Nick found his way to his feet again. It seemed to take an hour to get there. Broken glass crunched under his weight and the drenched carpet made squishing sounds as he turned to face his attacker. He ran one hand over his buzzcut, and his fingers came away smeared with blood, dirty water, and slimy strings of algae. A gritty rainbow of pink, blue, and purple pebbles was stuck to his palm.

Nick flicked a dead goldfish off his shoulder, and his already-mangled features twisted even further, into a scowl of disbelief.

"You gotta be kidding me."

Another dead fish went *pop!* beneath his boot.

"You hit me with an *aquarium*?"

Nick's attacker wore nothing but a pair of cut-off jean shorts and enormous plastic-framed glasses that magnified his eyes to cartoonish proportions. His hair fell to his shoulders in a mullet the color of old pennies. His ribs were visible above a sunken stomach that hinted of malnourishment. A few blotchy gray tattoos on his chest and arms resembled some flesh-eating disease that had decided after a little while that this guy just wasn't worth the trouble.

"Oh, Jeez...Jeezus, I'm...sorry," he stammered. His teeth were crooked and yellow.

He bolted for the doorway.

Nick lunged for him, but his reflexes weren't what they used to be. Not to mention the fact that he'd just had a fully-stocked fish tank dropped on his dome. He could feel the cuts in his scalp opening and closing with every move he made, like a hundred miniature mouths scolding him for coming here in the first place.

He staggered out of the room, saw a blur of flesh and denim fleeing through the front door.

Concussion or no concussion, no way was he gonna let this crazy fucker out of his sight.

Nick took off after him.

†

He stumbled out the front door and down the porch steps—his bad knee buckled on the last one, but by some miracle he didn't go down—just in time to see the guy's bony ass clearing the back corner of the house.

Blood and dirty water dripped from Nick's earlobes, down his chin. The evening's cool breeze raised a rash of goosebumps on his wet skin. He fought to keep up, but his sense of balance was off-kilter, and his quarry had gotten a head start of at least a hundred feet.

The guy glanced back over his shoulder before plunging into the woods at the rear of the property.

Nick followed. Low-hanging branches slapped at him like the hands of jilted ex-lovers. Briars tore at his arms.

Then something caught the big man's eye up ahead. A glint of sunlight off metal.

As he drew closer, he could see what it was: a crooked mobile home in the middle of the woods.

"I just wanna talk to you, fella!" Nick shouted. "Will you hold on a damn second?"

The guy glanced back again, tripped. Ate a faceful of forest floor. He wasted no time getting back to his feet, but in the meantime Nick closed the distance between them by half.

The trees thinned out. Nick followed his quarry onto a plot of red-brown earth adjacent to a corner of that cow pasture he had driven by earlier. In the center of the clearing sat a small green and white singlewide. Looked like it might blow away if someone let loose a powerful sneeze in its vicinity. Its battered aluminum body was speckled all over with patches of rust. Leaning against one side of the trailer was a mud-spattered moped; a dented yellow helmet hung from its handlebars.

Between the east end of the mobile home and the pasture's barbed-wire fence sat an old doghouse. Judging from the leaf-filled food bowl in its doorway, it had been abandoned for quite some time.

Nick slowed, but continued across the yard. Fought the urge to wince from the pain throbbing through his left knee.

The skinny man paused before a stack of milk crates that were the trailer's makeshift front steps. He turned to face Nick, and his mouth fell open as if he wanted to say something. But he didn't.

Nick held one hand out toward him. "Easy, now. I just wanna talk."

The stranger glanced up at the front door of his trailer. Back at Nick. The door. Nick.

"You just wanna talk?" His sunken chest heaved in and out, in and out. "Promise you're not gonna hurt me?"

"Make another move like you did at the house, I will defend myself," said Nick. "Otherwise, I won't lay a hand on you."

The man's bony shoulders slumped. "Hell. Ain't like I got anywhere to go from here. You might as well come on in."

He climbed the milk-crate steps, motioned for Nick to follow.

"Welcome to my humble commode, Mr. Bullman. I know it don't look like much, but it's home."

✝

The trailer's foundation creaked and groaned beneath them like some slowly-dying beast. Nick prayed it would hold his weight. Wasn't too keen on his odds.

The place smelled like mildew, marijuana, cigarettes, and beer. Draped across the back wall of the living room was a massive skull-and-crossbones flag. Beneath the flag sat a babyshit-yellow sofa. Dog-eared *Hustler* and *Heavy Metal* magazines covered the surface of a crooked coffee table, along with several empty beer cans, a pack of rolling papers, and an overflowing ashtray shaped like a steer skull. A short bar constructed of cheap particleboard separated the living room from the kitchen. Leaning against the end of the bar was a stereo system with most of its knobs missing and speakers that looked as if they had been mauled by mountain lions.

Nick couldn't help what he was thinking as he took in his surroundings. This place made his shithole apartment back in Memphis look like the Taj Mahal.

He turned to see the skinny man rummaging through a mountain of dirty clothes in one corner of the living room.

Any worries he might have had about the guy whirling on him with a weapon in hand vanished from his mind as quickly as they came. Despite the stunt with the fish tank, he was pretty sure this fellow was harmless. He could break the weirdo in half if he wanted. Throw him for a mile with little effort. Besides, the other man was so consumed right now with whatever he was doing, it was as if Nick wasn't even there.

He picked up a pair of crusty-looking jeans, tossed them aside.

Next a pair of brown-streaked underwear flew through the air, landed atop the porn rags on the coffee table.

Nick crossed his arms, raised one gnarled eyebrow. "You wanna tell me what's going on? And how the hell do you know my name?"

"Wait, I think this is it!" The guy pulled a black T-shirt from the pile of dirty clothes, turned it inside-out. MOTORHEAD, read the logo on the front. "Shit...I know it's in here somewhere!"

Yet another unwashed article of clothing landed on the floor at Nick's feet. He stepped back, so it was no longer touching the toe of his boot. Was that a plus-size *corset*?

"Bingo!"

These days, Nick Bullman went through life with a drooping, lipless mouth that resembled nothing so much as a razor-slit in a piece of raw meat. But he couldn't help himself: both corners of that slit curled upward into a ghastly grin when he saw what the skinny man had been so eager to show him.

A skull-faced figure leered at him from the front of the shirt. Its hair hung to its waist, and its muscular arms were raised in victory. The demon stood in the middle of a wrestling ring consumed by flames.

The skinny man flipped the shirt around.

THE WIDOWMAKER ATE MY SOUL!!! read the slogan on the back, above a list of cities and tour dates.

"I was *there*, man. Louisville, Kentucky. Front fuckin' row! I even got some o' your blood on me when Father Ivan Ruffstuff threw you outta the ring durin' your Thumbtacks-and-Broken-Glass Brawl! It was the greatest night of my *life!*"

Nick barely stifled the deep chuckle that threatened to slip out of him. "What's your name, fella?"

"Leon. My name's Leon." The guy pointed at Nick with one long, filthy-nailed finger. "And you're Nick Bullman, A.K.A. the Widowmaker."

"How about you just call me Nick for now?"

"Nick. Right. You got it." The guy bounced on his heels like a hyperactive child waiting to climb aboard his favorite amusement park ride. "Melissa said you was her pop, but I thought she was pullin' my dick. I never woulda th—"

"You know Melissa?" Nick interrupted him.

"I mean, we never talked too much, but I'd see her comin' and goin'. Man, I sure am sorry for hittin' you like that. You know your head's still bleedin'? I wish I had some Band-Aids. But I don't."

"I'll live," said Nick.

"I'm so stupid! I finally get to meet you, and I fuck it up. I can't do nothin' right!"

"Forget it. That's not important right now. Leon, I need you to tell me—"

"You don't understand, dude. I was your number one fan! I bought all your videos, owned every action figure. I even had the one they discontinued, with your upside-down-cross makeup? Too bad my dog got hold of it. We had this weiner dog when I was a kid, he died chokin' on it. That thing'd probably be worth, like, a million dollars now! The toy, I mean, not the dog. One time when I was in junior high, my old man beat me up so bad I had to learn how to write left-handed, after he found out I stole thirty bucks outta his wallet. It was worth the ass-whuppin', though. I needed the dough so I could join your fan club."

Nick had reached the limits of his patience. "I'm flattered, Leon. I am. But I need to talk to you about the night Eddie Whiteside was murdered. About what happened to Melissa's daughter. You were their closest neighbor. Maybe you saw something that night?"

Leon appeared deeply wounded by Nick's apathy toward hearing more tales of his lifelong Widowmaker worship. But was there something *else* in his expression? Nick was quite sure he saw *fear* in the other man's eyes as well, at the mention of Eddie's murder.

"First things first, I need to know what you were doing over there. That house is private property. Not to mention a crime scene, in case you hadn't noticed."

Leon said nothing for the next minute or so. He just stood there, gnawing at his dirty fingernails. His jittery gaze shot toward the door as if he was considering making another run for it.

Finally, he pulled the Widowmaker shirt over his bony torso and gave a defeated sigh.

"I need a smoke. How about we take a load off, I'll tell you everything I know."

To which Nick replied, "Best idea I've heard all day."

†

The kitchen's linoleum floor might have once been white; now it was piss-colored, scuffed and sticky. A small card table sat in the middle of the room, two folding chairs on either side of it. The tabletop was littered with old fast-food wrappers, dirty dishes, and empty beer cans.

Leon plucked a pack of cigarettes off the bar. Slid a Zippo lighter from the ass pocket of his shorts, lit up. "Can I get you a cold beer?"

He said "cold beer" as if it were one word—*coldbeer.*

"Why not," said Nick.

The refrigerator rattled and quaked as Leon opened it up. He scrounged around in there so long Nick started to wonder if he had climbed inside of it to hide. Taped to the fridge's door was a wrinkled centerfold: a red-headed woman with a lazy eye lay spread-eagle on the floor of an auto-repair shop; with one pink-nailed hand she was inserting a small wrench into a place normally reserved for tools of a more sterile nature.

At last, Leon tossed his hero a can of Milwaukee's Best.

He plopped down into one of the dented metal chairs at the table.

Nick sat across from him.

They sipped at their coldbeers for a minute or two.

Suddenly, Leon erupted with a shrill noise that was part lunatic giggle, part whooping redneck cheer. "Pinch me, 'cause I gotta be dreamin'. The Widowmaker is sittin' in my kitchen!"

He knocked over his beer. It foamed out on the table. He blushed, set the can upright in time to salvage half of it.

Nick said, "You know those days are long gone, right? I'm not the Widowmaker anymore."

"You'll always be 'Maker to me, man. The greatest grappler who ever lived!"

"I appreciate that. But—"

"I coulda killed them sons-a-bitches for what they did to you. I followed your recovery in the rasslin' mags. Kept up with the trial too, after you choked out McDouchebag. Man, that was awesome!"

"It wasn't as 'awesome' as you think," said Nick. "I lost my cool. It cost me everything."

Leon puffed on his cigarette, waved one skinny arm around his home. "Yeah, well. It can't be worse than this, can it?"

Nick finished off his beer. Crushed the can in one hand. "You wanna tell me what you were looking for back at the house?"

Leon made a face like he had bitten into something sour. His bloodshot eyes looked larger than ever behind his glasses. Nick could hear him grinding his teeth.

"No more bullshit, Leon. Time to start talking. Now."

"It's kinda embarrassin'."

"I won't judge."

"I got this problem, see. A monkey on my back."

"You were looking for drugs," said Nick.

Leon hung his head, exhaled smoke through his nose.

Nick sat back, allowed him to tell his story even when he wanted to put the guy in a full-nelson headlock and roar: *Would you get to the fucking point?*

"Two years ago, my old lady walked out on me. I was a wreck. We'd been together for six years. I was workin' for this septic tank company, always came home smellin' like other people's shit. Vonda hated it, said there had to be something better out there. I guess she found him. Last time I seen her, she'd hooked up with this Mexican fixes lawnmowers for a livin'.

"Wasn't long after she dumped my ass I started messin' around with meth. I ain't proud of it, but it's true. I quit the shit-tank gig, started workin' graveyard over at the plastics plant. I was pullin' double shifts, thought maybe I could save up some money and buy Vonda back. I tried to tell myself at first that I was just snortin' the stuff to stay awake on the job—one time I didn't sleep for *twelve days straight*, hoss—but the truth is, when I was tweakin' I didn't have a care in the world. Nothin' mattered anymore except where that next bag o' buzzard dust was comin' from."

Leon took a long drag off his cigarette.

"Your son-in-law, Eddie? He was the one who introduced me to the stuff."

"He wasn't my son-in-law," said Nick.

"Anyway...he used to sell it. I guess that was a convenient arrangement for both of us, seein' how we was neighbors."

Nick said, "I also suspect it's what got his head blown off."

Once again, Leon had a hard time meeting the big man's eyes. His hand trembled as he dropped his unfinished cigarette in a dirty cereal bowl. Its fire went out with a hiss.

"I figured the pigs cleaned out Eddie's place, but maybe they missed somethin'. The sheriff had a patrol car watchin' the house nonstop, the first couple weeks after what happened. Once it was gone, I couldn't help myself, dude! I've been jonesin' bad. Swear to God I was gonna put everything back like I found it. I didn't mean no disrespect to your kin. I just wanted to get spun."

"I don't give a damn about any of that," said Nick. "All I care about is helping Melissa find her daughter."

Leon fidgeted in his chair.

"You saw something the night Eddie was killed, didn't you, Leon? You saw something, and it scared the hell out of you."

"I keep to myself, hoss. Mind my own business."

"Back at the house, you thought I was someone else."

"You snuck up on me! I panicked, that's all. Thought you mighta been one of Sheriff Mackey's men."

"You're lying."

"Nope."

"I'm asking for your help, Leon. You'd tell me the truth, if you were half the 'Maker fan you claim to be."

"Dude! That ain't playin' fair!"

Nick couldn't resist: "I always did hit below the belt."

"Okay!" Leon sank in his chair. "I seen 'em! I seen 'em, but I didn't say nothin' 'cause I was scared I'd end up like Eddie!"

"Tell me what happened."

"I was out in the pasture, lookin' for 'shrooms. Fella I know told me that could be a lucrative gig, diggin' through cowshit, sellin' what you find. This musta been 'round one-thirty in the mornin'. All of a sudden, I heard tires squealin'. Car doors slammin'. Buncha cussin' and shoutin'. I snuck through the woods to see what was goin' on...and that's when I heard the shotgun blast."

"Go on."

"Four of 'em came out of the house. Two big bastards—like, your size, almost—and two smaller ones. They had Melissa's kid."

"And then?"

"They threw her in the back of their car, took off."

"She was struggling, trying to get away?"

"Oh, she put up a hell of a fight. She got one of the big dudes good, clawed him in the face."

"Would you recognize these guys if you saw them again?"

"It was dark. They was wearin' suits and ties, I think. But no, I couldn't make out their faces."

"What kind of car was it?"

"Somethin' fancy-lookin'. Black. Or maybe blue."

"That narrows it down."

Leon snickered, but his laugh turned into a choking sound in the back of his throat when he realized his hero wasn't trying to be funny.

"The cops think Sophie killed him," Nick said.

"I heard about that."

"But you never told them what you witnessed."

Leon started scratching furiously at his left nipple. "Like I said, I was scared they'd come after me if I started blabbin' about what I'd seen. Them guys looked like mobsters or somethin', kinda dudes who'd just as soon put you in a pair of concrete boots and dump you in the Snake River as look at ya. On top of that, me and the fuzz ain't exactly the best of friends."

"That's a shock."

"I reckon I shoulda called somebody, but—"

"You're damn right, you should have. I can't believe it's been *three weeks* and you've kept this to yourself the whole time?"

"I'm sorry," Leon whined. He murmured something to himself that the big man couldn't hear. A prayer, perhaps.

Nick took a deep breath, let it out slowly.

"I'll do anything I can to make it up to you, man, I sw—"

"Shut up a minute. Lemme think."

"I'll help you find her."

"I said shut up."

Leon mimed zipping his lips shut.

Finally, Nick calmed himself. He took another deep breath. "Say you'll do anything?"

"S-Sure, man. Whatever you need!"

"Give me a number where I can reach you over the next few days."

"Uhh...that might be a problem, hoss. I don't have a phone. I used to. But I was tweakin' one night, took it apart. Afterwards I couldn't figure out how to put it back together."

Nick rubbed at his temples. "Jesus Christ."

When his hero finally stood, Leon looked relieved, as if he could barely believe he had survived this exchange.

"You takin' off?"

"Gonna head back to my motel room, touch base with Melissa. Probably need to have a chat with the local law as well."

"You gonna tell them what I told you? About what I seen that night?"

"Count on it."

"Fuck me runnin'." Leon started gnawing at his fingernails again. "I'm a dead man."

"You're not a dead man."

"Sure as I'm sittin' here. Might as well just find me a hole somewhere, lay down in it and pull the dirt in over my head."

Nick said, "Trust me. You've done the right thing."

"For once in my sorry-ass life?"

"You said it, not me."

Leon laughed.

Nick didn't. He turned to leave, glad to finally get out of there.

†

Evening. Nick headed back to town. Beyond the Blue Ridge Mountains bordering Polk County, the horizon had turned the color of ripe peaches.

He spotted the black-and-white the second he pulled into the parking lot of the Sunrise Motor Lodge. It was parked conspicuously in front of the motel's main office. A man in a khaki uniform leaned against the patrol car, talking into a cellphone.

The Bronco's brakes whined as Nick backed the vehicle into a spot facing his room.

In his peripheral vision he saw the lawman cut his call short, start walking toward him. Nick took his time switching off the ignition. Rolling up the windows. Dabbing at his leaking eyeball. Pocketing his keys, then sliding the fob for Room 118 out of the ashtray where he had stashed it.

He got out of the truck. Slammed the door.

"Mr. Bullman? Nick Bullman?"

The man with the badge was in his early forties. His hair was close-cropped at his temples, just starting to turn gray. He had a muscular frame, but carried a hint of a middle-age belly, as if he might have once pumped iron but had gotten out of the habit the last few years. He wore a five o'clock shadow, wire-rimmed glasses with a blue tint.

"Sheriff Kyle Mackey," he introduced himself.

"Sheriff," said Nick.

The cop's handshake was firm, sincere. "I was wondering if I might have a few words with you."

"We do need to talk," Nick said. "You wanna come on in the room?"

"Actually, I was thinking we could head over to the Denny's on Brookshire Boulevard." When Nick didn't say anything, the sheriff lowered his voice as if he and the big man were coconspirators. "Had to skip breakfast this morning. Any time that happens, I get cranky. Have to make up for it later in the day. It's my favorite meal."

Nick couldn't care less about the sheriff's eating habits. But they did have a lot to talk about.

"What do you say? Denny's, my treat?"

"I've never been one to turn down a free meal," said Nick.

"Good man," said the sheriff. "We'll take my car."

✝

They started off with idle conversation—talk about the weather, and about how much Midnight had changed in the last thirty years—and Nick noticed the whole time that the sheriff seemed to have no reservations about looking into his disfigured face as they spoke. He wasn't used to this. Folks *always* reacted one of two ways: with an anything-but-subtle aversion to his mug...or they couldn't tear their eyes off of it, as if he were some scientific anomaly.

Not this guy, though. Sheriff Kyle Mackey had honed his poker face to perfection. Done his homework beforehand, most likely, knew what to expect upon meeting the man who had once been the Widowmaker.

"I'll get to the point," the sheriff said between bites of his long-awaited breakfast. "In a place like Midnight, word travels fast. I heard you were in town, thought it'd be best if I wasted no time making sure we're on the same page."

Nick took a sip of his iced tea. "Say what you gotta say, Sheriff."

Mackey put down his fork. Nick noticed a stripe of pale skin on his left ring finger, where the lawman had once worn a wedding band.

"I'm asking you not to get involved in this. With all due respect, I need you to stay out of my way, let me do my job."

"What makes you think I'd want to get in your way?" Nick said.

"Mr. Bullman, I wasn't born yesterday. I know Melissa is desperate. She must have asked you to—"

"Since when is it a crime to visit my daughter?"

"I never said it was."

"The poor girl's on the verge of a nervous breakdown. She's got nobody."

"Finding Sophie is my number one priority, Mr. Bullman." Mackey rested his elbows on the tabletop. "I've got every man in my department pulling double-time seven days a week to bring Sophie home. The SBI has been called in on this. We're utilizing resources from the National Center for Missing and Exploited Children. All I'm asking is, you don't do anything to muddy up my investigation."

Nick let him finish.

"We're on the same side here, make no mistake. On the other hand, if you get in my way I will not hesitate to do whatever I have to do to move you aside."

"Fair enough."

The sheriff dug back into his breakfast. "Glad we understand one another."

"I gotta wonder, though, how well this 'investigation' of yours is going, considering it's been almost a month," said Nick. "From what I hear, you're no closer to finding Melissa's daughter than you were the night she disappeared."

Sheriff Mackey froze with his fork an inch or two from his mouth. He knew he'd been insulted. But before he had a chance to retort, a pretty young waitress approached their table.

"Freshen up your coffee, Sheriff?"

"Thank you, Sandra."

The waitress stared at a spot somewhere over Nick's left shoulder. "Sir? More tea?"

"Sure. Thanks."

She looked disappointed, as if the big man had let her down. She snatched up his glass and took it away.

"You've got nothing, Sheriff," Nick said the instant she was out of earshot, "because you've been looking at this all wrong from the start."

Mackey set down his fork. Stared at Nick.

"You think Sophie did it," said Nick. "You think she murdered this drug-dealing piece of shit."

"It's one theory," said the sheriff. "It's certainly not the only one."

"Well, it's dead wrong."

"Mr. Bullman, whether you or your daughter choose to believe it or not, there is *no* evidence to suggest there was anyone in the house with Eddie that night except Sophie. Plus, I've got a phone call from Sophie *telling* Melissa she did it. I'm supposed to ignore that because no one wants to believe a fourteen-year-old is capable of doing something like this? Kids younger than that commit murder all the time, without provocation."

"Wait a minute. What *phone call* are you talking about?"

"Your daughter must have told you."

"I guess she didn't."

"We put a tap on her phone for the first couple of days after Sophie went missing, hoping that we might get a ransom call. I never expected anything to come of it, given Melissa's financial situation, but it is standard procedure. About forty-eight hours in, Sophie called her mother from a payphone in Hendersonville."

"That doesn't make any sense," said Nick.

"She told Melissa that Eddie had been putting his filthy hands on her since she first came to live with them. She assured her that she was safe, and promised she would be in touch again 'as soon as things died down'."

Nick shook his head, refused to believe what he was hearing. "Someone *forced* her to make that call. My granddaughter was kidnapped. I have proof."

The sheriff gave a mildly annoyed expression, but his eyebrows rose behind his tinted glasses. He wanted to hear more.

Nick obliged him. He filled Mackey in on everything Leon had told him, about four men forcing Sophie into a fancy black car. He wasn't sure why, but he chose *not* to rat Leon out in regards to his breaking into Eddie's house, searching for drugs. Perhaps he felt he'd gained an unlikely confidante in the twitchy little speed freak? Plus, there was the matter of his own illegal entry. He changed the details of how they had met to a vague white-lie account of the skinny man walking out of the woods, striking up a conversation while Nick's Bronco sat idling in front of

Melissa's former home.

The sheriff was suddenly uninterested in finishing his favorite meal. He pushed his plate aside, slid a pen and a small notepad from his breast pocket.

"Leon Purdy," he said, as he scribbled something on the pad. "Assuming the little scumbag was telling you the truth, this changes everything. Why hasn't he come forward with this information before now?"

"He was scared. And Leon claims his relationship with local law enforcement is...strained."

"He ain't seen nothing yet," said the sheriff. "Son of a bitch."

The waitress returned with Nick's tea. Ice cubes clinked against the inside of the glass as she set it in front of him.

"Sandra, can you bring the check?" Mackey was already dropping a few dollar bills on the table for her tip, preparing to scoot out of the booth. "I've gotta roll."

†

Melissa picked up the phone halfway through its third ring. Several seconds passed before she mumbled into it, "Hello?"

Nick couldn't tell whether she sounded half-asleep because he had woke her, or perhaps she had taken something to ease her mental anguish since he saw her last.

According to the clock on his motel room nightstand, the time was a few minutes past eight p.m.

"Melissa, it's Nick. We need to talk."

"What's going on?" Instantly, she was wide-awake. "Did you find out anything new?"

"I met your neighbor."

"Leon?"

"That's the guy."

"Leon's an idiot."

"I noticed."

He heard the *shnick* of a lighter on her end of the line.

"I walked in on him tossing your bedroom. Trying to find Eddie's stash."

"What a loser." She didn't sound surprised, though. "It's not the first time he's pulled this shit."

"No?"

"About a year ago we came home to find him standing in our hallway bathroom. He'd pulled the lid off the toilet tank. Looked like a kid caught with his hand in the cookie jar. Except in this case it was Leon with his hand in our crapper, blue up to his arms."

"Jesus."

"Why are we talking about that dumbass, anyway? What does Leon have to do with any of this?"

"Turns out he was my 'number one fan' back in the day. But he got nervous as hell when I brought up Eddie's murder. He saw something that night, I was sure of it. So I put the pressure on him, got him talking."

"And?"

"Melissa, do you think Eddie might have had ties to organized crime?"

"You're talking about the *mob*? This is Midnight. Stuff like that doesn't go on here."

"Fourteen-year-old girls aren't supposed to disappear either," said Nick.

She didn't say anything.

"How about the people he associated with? Any idea where he got his drugs?"

"He never told me. I never asked. I must have seen some of the same faces drop by the house now and then. I remember this one black guy who always seemed to make Eddie nervous. But I never knew their names. I didn't *want* to know them."

"Think you would recognize any of those people if you saw them again?"

"Maybe. Probably not. Usually he just met them out at the curb. He never invited them inside. Why?"

"Leon was hiding in the woods the night Eddie was killed. He saw four men come out of the house. They had Sophie."

"I knew it!" She started sobbing. "Oh, my baby..."

"Melissa, it's gonna be okay. I promise." But even as he said it, Nick wondered: *Where do I get off promising her* anything? *For all I know, her kid is already dead, buried in a shallow grave somewhere off I-26...*

Neither of them said anything for the next few seconds. He heard her draw deeply on her cigarette several times, then exhale slowly. Trying to calm herself.

"I spoke with the sheriff," Nick said. "He's looking into Leon's story."

"Good. That's good."

"He said Sophie called you, two days after she went missing. Why didn't you tell me that?"

"I'm sorry," she said. "I wasn't trying to be dishonest with you. I just...I left that part out 'cause I didn't want you thinking the same thing the cops have been thinking all this time. Somebody *forced* her to make that call. I could hear it in my baby's voice. It sounded like she was reading off a piece of paper, like a script. They told her what to say. I know they did!"

"After talking to Leon, I think you're right," Nick said. "The men who took her, they knew Eddie, figured it wouldn't be much of a stretch for the cops to believe he would molest a little girl. But listen to me, Melissa. If I'm gonna try to help you find her, you can't be keeping things from me."

"It won't happen again," she said.

"I don't like surprises. Another thing...you should trust the sheriff to do what he gets paid to do. He seems like a good man. He's just in over his head with all of this."

"It's only 'cause of Sheriff Mackey that I never ended up in some kind of juvie hall when I was a teenager," Melissa said. "He used to feel sorry for Mom, I think. I got picked up for shoplifting and underage drinking more times than I can count, but every time he'd just lecture me and take me back home. A few days after Sophie disappeared, I made a huge scene at the diner, in front of half the town. Accused him of not doing his job. I threw my Coca-Cola at him. He just sat there and took it. I know he's doing his best to find Sophie. But it's hard, Daddy. It's so damn hard."

He heard her blow her nose on the other end of the line.

When that was done, she said, "Eddie hated Sheriff Mackey. Of course. He was a drug dealer. It's the natural order of things, right?"

"Did Mackey ever arrest him?" Nick asked.

"Yeah. The last time was earlier this year. That one was a close call, 'cause of the 'three strikes' law. He already had two strikes against him, from a few years before we met. It was during a routine traffic stop. But he had just come back from a big sell that day, so all they found in his truck was a little weed and some paraphernalia. Misdemeanor possession. Eddie said the Man Upstairs must have been watching out for him."

Nick felt a hot rush of aggravation. Not only toward her late boyfriend, but a little toward Melissa as well. He didn't stop to consider her feelings before he said what he said next.

"If they'd thrown his ass in prison, he would still be alive. Your daughter would be sitting there beside you. If the Man Upstairs had anything to do with it, I'm afraid He didn't think things through."

†

It had been a long, strange day. An afternoon of dark discoveries and bizarre revelations. Now that it was over Nick planned to sit for a while, take the quiet time to sort it all out.

"I'm a *grandfather*."

The words didn't sound right on his lips. As if he spoke some foreign phrase with which he was vaguely familiar but its meaning alluded him.

"*Grampa. Grandaddy. Pappaw...*"

He chuckled, shook his head as he sprawled out on his lumpy motel bed.

A minute or two later, his chainsaw snore filled the room.

†

Nick Bullman dreamed.

He dreamed of friendly cops talking with their mouths full...of chain-smoking daughters with wet, swollen eyes...he dreamed of bony meth-heads...of adolescents abducted by shadow-men in fancy suits... and he dreamed of no-good boyfriends dealing drugs and playing pimp, before their heads disappeared in explosions of blood and brain and bits of shattered white skull.

In his dreams, as in reality, Nick felt so useless. He was a passive observer cuffed with cold steel to something immovable while blurry figures removed his flesh with a blade the size of a Buick.

He awoke about the time Lance K. McDougal III appeared in his dream. Vengeance burned in the billionaire's eyes as he hefted a shotgun, pointed it at Nick's face...

He ratcheted the weapon.

It was the loudest sound Nick had ever heard.

Loud enough to startle him from sleep.

And once he was awake he realized the sound had not come from his dream at all.

JAMES NEWMAN 61

†

The room was dark. *Too* dark...

A shape stood between Nick and the glow of the parking lot lights outside his motel room window. A human shape.

As his vision came into focus, he realized he was staring down the eye of a *gun barrel.*

Nick heaved his bulk to the left.

The gun barked out a sharp *POP!*, and a hole appeared in the pillow where his head had lain a second before. Bits of stuffing floated up into the air like heavy snowflakes.

He rolled off of the bed, onto the floor, came down hard on his bad knee as the gunman pulled the trigger twice more: *POP! POP!*

Nick spat out a four-letter word or twelve. A nerve twitched in the crook of his neck as he crawled forward, risking a glance around the corner of the bed.

Gradually, his eyes adjusted to the darkness. He could see now that the shooter was a short, stocky man in his late forties. He wore a dark suit with a western-style bolo tie. Salt-and-pepper mutton-chop sideburns framed a hint of a double chin. The gun in his hand was fitted with a silencer.

From where Nick lay, he could smell the guy's cologne. A hint of liquor, too. The fragrance was something expensive. The hooch was not.

When the hitman spoke to Nick, his voice was almost kind. As if he wasn't proud of what he had come here to do but he had no choice.

"This has to happen, big fella. Nothing you can do to stop it."

Nick clung to the floor, his heart thudding in his chest.

"If it's any consolation, the kid don't want for nothing. But she belongs to Daddy now. And he is *very* protective of his property."

"What the fuck?" Nick whispered to himself.

He watched the hitman's fancy shoes round the bed.

"Now, how about you make this easier for both of us? Lie still, I'll put one in the back of your head, and you won't ever see it coming."

Nick said, "Oh. Well. Since you put it that way—"

He rose, leapt over the bed.

The gunman had stopped to take a swig from a small metal flask. He dropped his drink, let out a startled yelp as three hundred pounds of ex-wrestler landed on top of him. His pistol fired off another shot, grazing

Nick's left shoulder. Glass shattered as the bullet struck a piece of cheap motel art on the wall.

"Where is she?" Nick roared.

He showed the fucker his best right hook.

Blood streamed from the hitman's nose, down his chin. Nick pinned his gun hand to the floor, hit him again.

"Tell me who sent you!"

In the room next door, someone pounded on the wall. A deep voice threatened to call the fuckin' popo.

The hitman kneed Nick in the balls.

Nick groaned, clutched himself through his sweatpants. Rolled off of his assailant.

The man in the suit stood. One hand went to his broken nose. The other trembled as it aimed the gun at Nick again.

Nick tasted puke rising in his gorge. *Get up, get up NOW unless you want to DIE!* But the boulder of agony that had planted itself in his abdomen allowed him to rise only as far as his hands and knees.

The assassin thumbed back the hammer on his gun.

And then the two men heard a knock. So soft it was nearly inaudible.

The door to Nick's room creaked open.

The giant and his would-be killer watched a shaft of bluish light sneak in through the doorway.

A rasping voice entered with it, a voice that obviously belonged to an elderly person: "What in the name of sweet Mother Mary is going on in here?"

The gunman pressed the hot tip of his pistol against Nick's forehead. He said nothing, but the message was clear: *Don't move. Don't even breathe.*

The geezer flicked on the light switch, and his ancient, dried-apple features went slack at the scene before him.

Nick blinked. So did the man standing over him.

Somewhere out on the interstate, an eighteen-wheeler's air-horn farted.

"Process server, my ass," the old man grumbled.

The hitman looked confused, like he was trying to decide what to do next.

He brought his gun up, pointed it at the motel manager.

Nick saw his only chance. Later, he would wonder if his next move might have been overkill. Probably. He outweighed his foe by at least a hundred pounds. But that knee in the balls had put him down for the count. Hard to think straight when it felt like someone had kicked your scrotum up into your throat.

When he had first checked in, he had dropped his wallet and keys on a table by the window. That stuff lay just a couple of feet away from him now, at eye level.

Nick snatched the key to his room off of the table. Thrust upward, with every ounce of strength left in him...

...and stabbed the key into his assailant's Adam's apple.

The guy staggered back. Dropped his gun. It fired one last shot when it hit the floor. The bullet whizzed past the manager, so close it lifted a tuft of his longish white hair as it *thunk*ed into the door.

The old man squealed, ducked, covered his head.

The hitman crashed into the television, clawing at his punctured windpipe as if everything would be okay if he could only figure out how to put it back together. He twirled, collided with a brass floor lamp, then fell into an overstuffed chair in the corner of the room. The noises coming out of him reminded Nick of the sounds the hogs used to make on his father's farm when he was a kid. The sounds they made when they were being slaughtered.

He rolled against the edge of the bed, laid there watching the man die.

It seemed to take forever.

Finally, he heard—and smelled—the shooter's bodily functions let go.

The guy looked nothing like a hired killer now. Just some middle-aged family man in his Sunday best, kicked back after a rough day at work. Only the bright red blood soaked into the front of his suit belied such a mundane image. His dead blue eyes stared up at the ceiling as if he were contemplating why he had come here at all.

He twitched once more—somehow the key had remained buried in his trachea throughout his dance of death, but with this final spasm it slid out of him as if retracted by an invisible hand, before tumbling into his lap—and then the hitman lay still.

"Call the sheriff," Nick said to the motel manager. "Now."

He went back to holding his balls, but only after using a boot to slide the dead man's flask across the carpet till it was close enough to grab.

There was still some liquor left inside. Nick helped himself to a long pull.

The manager clutched at his chest with one liver-spotted hand as he shambled out of the room, and Nick could hear him babbling something about a "shooting spree" all the way across the parking lot.

†

At just past one o'clock in the morning, the Sunrise Motor Lodge was a maelstrom of activity, an island of bright lights and noise in the center of a town that otherwise slept peacefully beneath the sea of a starless night sky.

Across the parking lot from where Nick stood next to his Bronco with Sheriff Mackey, two paramedics carried a body bag out of Room 118 and loaded it into a waiting ambulance. A dozen or so motel tenants lingered beyond the roped-off perimeter of the crime scene, their curious faces painted alternating shades of red and blue by the lights of the patrol cars on the property. Every few minutes, one of them—a bushy-haired man in pajama pants with a can of Pabst Blue Ribbon in his hand—hollered a question the investigators' way. The smell of another guest's cigar permeated the night air, along with the squawk of police radios. The shadows of everyone present stretched across the lot like bloodstains on the pavement.

The night was hot, sticky. The wound on Nick's left shoulder burned where the bullet had grazed him. The EMTs had dressed it for him earlier, and both of the young men had recommended stitches. But Nick assured them that he had lived through much worse. He pulled up his sleeve to check on it now, saw crimson blossoming through the bandage.

"No I.D. on our shooter," Sheriff Mackey said, as they watched the paramedics slam the double doors at the rear of the ambulance. His uniform was rumpled as if he had slept in it. "We'll run his prints through AFIS, the national database. We've matched every vehicle in the lot against the guest register. I'm assuming an accomplice dropped him off, planned to circle around and pick him up after the deed was done."

They watched the ambulance depart. No lights, no siren. Neither was necessary, considering where the van's passenger was headed.

"He had a pin-and-tumbler set in his jacket. Illegal to possess in the state of North Carolina without a locksmith license. We'll look into that, but I don't expect anything to come of it. Black market, most likely."

"He was an amateur," Nick said. "Carried the right tools, but this wasn't his thing."

"What makes you say that?"

"Once he's inside the room, he has me right where he wants me. He fires off multiple shots at pointblank range, and misses every time?"

"Doesn't make sense," the sheriff agreed.

"I think the booze was liquid courage. He hesitated. That's the only reason I'm standing here talking to you."

The sheriff looked off toward the crime scene, jingled some change in his pockets.

"From what I've heard about Eddie Whiteside's murder," said Nick, "it was sloppy too. Only difference is, shotgun makes a big boom. Whoever offed Eddie wasn't too worried about being heard out in the boonies. It was supposed to be quick, easy. Things didn't go as planned."

Nick sighed, ran one hand over the prickly gray hairs atop his skull. He watched a woman in a green business suit and tortoise-shell glasses walk out of his room carrying a clear plastic bag marked EVIDENCE. Even from where he stood, he could see what was inside the bag: the key to Room 118, coated in half-congealed blood.

Overhead, the big Sunrise Motor Lodge sign (**CLEAN ROOMs + Hb0 = $34.95/NITE**) made a ticking sound, then abruptly went dark. As if the manager had decided he couldn't handle any more business that might come rolling in tonight. Not after everything he'd been through. Nick glanced over toward the office, saw the old man speaking to a tall black cop; he was waving his hands about, looking distraught, while the deputy scribbled his statement in a notebook.

Nick thought about the bizarre things the hitman had said just before their fight. He debated whether or not he should tell the sheriff. Although he didn't really know why, he decided he would wait. Sit on it, and try to make sense of it himself before he shared it with anyone.

"Ask you a question, Sheriff?"

"What's that?"

"Who knows I'm here?"

"At the motel?"

"You know what I mean."

"Far as I know, there's just your daughter, myself, and your pal Leon Purdy. Why do you ask?"

"I've been in Midnight—ten, twelve hours? Already, someone's tried to take me out of the picture. I'd like to know how this asshole knew where to find me. *Exactly* where to find me."

Mackey said, "You're a hard fellow to miss, Mr. Bullman. I knew you were in town ten minutes after you walked into Annie's Country Diner."

"Right."

"I don't think I appreciate whatever it is you're insinuating."

"I'm not insinuating anything, Sheriff. Just thinking out loud."

Nick yawned. He didn't know why he had chosen to take the antagonistic route. But he couldn't help it. Waking up with a gun in your face tends to darken one's mood.

The sheriff turned, mumbled something into his walkie-talkie. An officer trotted over a minute later with two Styrofoam cups of coffee. He still had on his latex gloves. Sheriff Mackey took a cup. Nick declined, and not just because he saw flakes of dried blood on the guy's gloves.

The sheriff sipped at his coffee, made a satisfied sound in the back of his throat.

"Do you think this could be tied to organized crime?" Nick asked him.

"Around here?" Mackey seemed to get a kick out of that.

"I'm serious."

"Thought you were. The closest thing we have to 'organized crime' is the rare trailer-park meth lab that I'm proud to say we shut down the second I get wind of it. Solicitation at the truck stops off I-26. But if you're talking about something out of *The Godfather*? I can assure you that those kind of people do *not* congregate in Midnight, North Carolina."

"Suppose Eddie Whiteside owed some bad people a lot of money. What if my granddaughter was the collateral that paid off his debt?"

The sheriff sighed. "I will review the information supplied to us by Leon Purdy. After what happened to you tonight, I'd be a fool not to admit that this whole thing is more complex than I first thought. But I wish you would leave the detective work to me, sir."

"You've done a hell of a job so far," said Nick.

The sheriff chewed at his bottom lip. Looked like he'd love to pull out his Glock, spend the next few hours pistol-whipping Nick with it. He took a long sip at his coffee before he spoke again.

"We're gonna play it like that? Well then, my turn to ask you a question. You told me that, before yesterday evening, you never knew you had a granddaughter. I took this to mean your relationship with Melissa is estranged. Would that be a fair assessment?"

"It would be."

"How well do you trust your daughter, Mr. Bullman?"

Nick glared at the sheriff, did not reply.

"Melissa stands to gain a lot of money from Eddie Whiteside's death. She happens to be the sole beneficiary of an insurance policy Eddie took out on himself a month before he was murdered."

Nick clenched his teeth. Fought to keep his temper in check. The big man had no nose, but the two wide black holes in the center of his disfigured face flared with anger.

Sheriff Mackey said, "I'm not insinuating anything, by the way. Just thinking out loud."

Score one for the prick in the khaki uniform.

"Do you need anything else from me?" Nick said. "If not, I should probably start looking for another place to stay."

"You're free to go," the sheriff replied. "But...Mr. Bullman?"

"Huh?"

"A blind man could see we've got a clear case of self-defense here. However, pending a meeting with the D.A., I'm sure I'll need to speak with you again. Make yourself available?"

"I'm not going anywhere," said Nick. "I promised Melissa I'd help her. That's what I aim to do."

"Try the south end of Brookshire, up past the bowling alley. Couple decent motels out that way, shouldn't cost you an arm and a leg."

Mackey gave Nick a final once-over, before walking away.

Nick watched him join his fellow lawmen in Room 118, then climbed into his Bronco, feeling every second of his fifty-four years. He was sore all over. His bicep burned, his bad knee throbbed, and his groin ached as if someone had been standing on it for the last few days, maybe jumped up and down when they got bored.

He didn't see the motel manager approaching him until the guy rapped on his window with one bony knuckle.

He took his time rolling down the window. "What the hell do *you* want?"

"Thought I'd better tell ya, a'fore you take off...somebody's gonna have to pay for the damage in there."

"Beg your pardon?" said Nick.

"Me and the missus, we ain't exactly got money fallin' outta our buttholes. It's all we can do to break even runnin' this place most days. Somebody's gonna have to pay for the repairs."

"A man tried to kill me tonight," said Nick, "in case you missed it."

"Wasn't me. I just own the motel. Now, I know you wasn't the one doin' the shootin'. But after what you did to that fella, I don't see him gettin' up to pay me what I'm owed."

Nick couldn't believe what he was hearing. "How did he know what room I was in? Tell me that, old man. Hell, I'm surprised he had to pick the lock, somebody didn't *hand him a goddamn key...*"

The gruesome double entendre in his own statement—*hand him a key*—was not lost on Nick.

The senior citizen's gaze dropped to the cracked asphalt. He shifted his weight from one foot to the other.

"How much did he pay you?" said Nick.

"I ain't got no dog in this fight, buddy. I just own th—"

"You just own the motel. I got that."

The geezer gave up then. He stalked off, shaking his head as if he couldn't believe how he'd been conned.

Nick started the Bronco. It backfired. He got a wicked thrill out of seeing every cop on the premises flinch.

As he pulled out of the lot, he passed a white van with a satellite dish on its roof, CHANNEL 13 NEWS painted on its side. He said a silent prayer, thanked whoever might be listening that he'd gotten out of there just in time, didn't have to deal with *that* shit.

As he cruised through Midnight, down lonely back roads and side streets smothered in darkness, he kept an eye on his cracked rearview mirror.

Nick Bullman was tired. So tired. But after tonight he wondered if he would ever sleep again.

†

Eight hours had passed since the attempt on Nick's life. Early the next morning, he called Melissa to tell her what happened. Their conversation was brief, as she was on her way to work (she had quit her job at the bar a few days after Sophie went missing, and had recently gone back to pulling double shifts at the Waffle House). He assured his daughter that he was okay as she wept into the phone, and he promised her that he would continue to watch his back. Before they said their goodbyes, he asked for her Aunt Patty's number. She gave it to him, along with a warning that he had never been her aunt's favorite person. He told her he suspected as much, but after an attempt on his life he could handle just about anything.

"You've got a lot of nerve calling this number," Aunt Patty started berating him as soon as he identified himself. "You are a piece of work, you know that? All that money, all that fame, you're still nothing. You're the lowest of the low."

He allowed her to get it out of her system, didn't bother reminding her that both the money and the fame had said *adios* a few years ago.

"I guess we can all rest easy now that *you've* come rolling back into town. After all these years. Gonna fix everything! Think you'll solve the mystery, Nick? Gonna find that little girl, so we can all live happily ever after?"

In the background he could hear water running, clinking glassware. Sounded like she was washing dishes.

She sighed. "Look. I already told the police. I haven't heard from Sophie. I don't know where she is. I wish to God I did."

"Pat," said Nick, "did either Sophie or Melissa ever mention a man called 'Daddy'?"

"Never. There's one name that's always been missing from *both* of their lives."

He knew he had walked right into that one. It stung.

"Last time I called Melissa, she told me to eat shit and die. After all I've done for that girl. She's in denial. I don't know if it's because of some misguided loyalty to that dirtbag, even though he's dead now, or because she knows if Sophie really was the one who killed him she would have to admit to herself what had been going on in that house right under her nose."

"You think—"

"Eddie had been molesting that poor girl. And she decided she wasn't gonna take it anymore."

For the first time since Patty answered the phone, her tone softened toward the man who should have been her brother-in-law. Not much, but a little.

"Something wasn't right with him," she said. "He had an unhealthy interest in Sophie before he ever laid eyes on her."

"What do you mean?"

"He called asking to speak with her. Late April, early May this would've been, when Sophie still lived with me. I handed her the phone. I had met Eddie a couple times at that point, and he seemed decent enough. I didn't find out about all the stuff he was into till after he was dead. I assumed he was just calling to relay a message from Melissa. But then he called again. Two or three times after that."

"What did he want?"

"He kept begging Sophie to come to Midnight to live with them. He told her it was the one thing her mother wanted more than anything in the world. Wasn't too long after that, he got his wish."

Nick was stunned.

Everything Patty told him matched the sheriff's original theory. As did Sophie's call, when she had asked her mother not to come looking for her. But Sophie *didn't* leave home of her own free will that night. She left because she had been *taken*. By four men in suits, driving a fancy car.

How did those goons fit into all of this, if Sophie had pulled the trigger on Eddie? Why had he seemed so hell-bent on reuniting Melissa with her daughter, if not for the vile purpose the cops initially suspected?

Two plus two kept coming up five. Nick couldn't make the pieces fit together. Trying made his brain hurt.

Aunt Patty gave another loud sigh into the phone then.

"That's all I've got." She sounded tired. Defeated. "Now do me a favor, Nick. You never brought anything but heartache to Melissa and her mother. I'd appreciate it if you wouldn't call this number again."

"I'm sorry, Pat," he said. "For everything. If I could go back—"

"I'm tempted to say you deserve what happened to you, and I'm glad they took your face. But that wouldn't be very Christian of me. So I won't."

She hung up.

✝

Later that morning, Nick trudged through the forest behind his daughter's former home, once again approaching Leon Purdy's crooked trailer. He wore a scuffed brown leather jacket, an old gray stocking cap. Twigs and dead pinecones crunched beneath his boots.

"Leon!" he called out. "You home?"

He didn't want to spook the little weirdo. Good way to end up...*with an aquarium dropped on your head?* Nick couldn't help chuckling as he thought of their first encounter. The look on Leon's face when he realized he had assaulted his hero! He wouldn't forget that any time soon.

The stench of cow manure tickled his nostrils. From somewhere on the far side of the pasture adjacent to Leon's property, Nick heard laughter, the stop-and-go buzz of some kids on a four-wheeler. A crow cawed from the branches of a massive oak tree, before swooping down to claim the remains of some small forest creature that had crawled under Leon's trailer to die. As its beak dipped and tore into the carrion, the bird's obsidian eyes watched Nick suspiciously, as if the giant human might try to make off with its prize.

Nick heard music coming from inside the trailer. He climbed the milk-crate steps, knocked on the dented front door. It swung open.

"Leon?"

He ducked through the doorway. Felt the mobile home tremble beneath his weight.

From the battered stereo system by the bar came the raucous din of death metal: squealing guitars, machine-gun drumming, and a singer who sounded like Satan himself wired on PCP.

Nick instantly had a headache. He wasted no time crossing the room, turning the music off.

"Leon?"

A shout from the opposite end of the trailer. "That you, Nick?"

"It's me."

"Make yourself at home!"

Nick was somehow able to find an uncluttered spot on the sofa.

"Be out in a minute, dude. You caught me droppin' some friends off at the pool."

"What's that?" Nick said, distracted. He swatted at a big green fly that was buzzing around his head, bouncing off the bandage on his bicep.

"Takin' the Browns to the Super Bowl."

"You lost me."

"Do I gotta spell it out for you, hoss? I'm takin' a shit!"

Nick groaned. As if the cigarettes-and-mildew stink of this place wasn't endearing enough already.

He heard toilet paper being rolled off its spool. Enough to last a family of six for a month, from the sound of it. The toilet flushed.

Nick shifted in his seat, breathed through his nose. "You almost done in there?"

After what felt like forever, Leon came strutting down the hall, zipping up his cut-off shorts. Today his scrawny torso was covered in a loud yellow T-shirt that read: GIMME HEAD TILL I'M DEAD.

"You ever wondered why they call it *takin'* a shit? To me that implies walkin' away with more than you had when you started. I prefer to *leave* it. Ha!"

Nick shook his head.

Leon nodded toward the silenced stereo. "What's the matter, bro? You didn't like my music?"

"Sorry," said Nick. "Not my thing."

Leon looked disappointed. "Them was the guys did your entrance theme back in the day. You remember?" He arched his back, played a few licks of furious air guitar, and sang badly, *"Gonna make your wife a widowwww, gonna send you six feet underrr!"*

"I remember it," said Nick. "Heard it every night for twenty-five years. I don't normally listen to that kind of music, though."

"You're pullin' my dick."

"I wouldn't think of doing that."

"What do you listen to?"

"Blues, mostly. More my speed."

"The blues is alright, I guess."

"It's the only music that's real," said Nick. "Where it all began."

Leon stared off into space, as his drug-addled brain tried to work that out. "So, anyway...to what do I owe the pleasure? Somethin' I can do for ya, brother? What happened to your arm?"

"Leon, I need your help."

"I'd love to help you, dude. Whatever you need. Did I tell you I always was your number one fan?"

"You might have mentioned it."

"How about a coldbeer?"

"No. Listen..."

Leon went to the fridge, got himself one. He slurped at it as he leaned against the bar and gave Nick his full attention.

"I'm gonna need you to be my second set of eyes," said Nick.

"Okay...?"

Nick stood, joined Leon in the kitchen. "A lot has changed in Midnight since the last time I was here. It's not as easy as it used to be for me to get out and talk to people. Plus, you know about this town's dark side. The things that crawl beneath the surface. You can get to information that it might not be so easy for Sheriff Mackey to come by."

"I'll try my best," Leon said.

"Eddie was a dealer. But he wasn't the only link in the chain. He got his product from a supplier."

Leon said, "Right..."

"His boss. Any idea who that might have been?"

"No idea, man. When I needed a bump, I always went through Eddie."

Nick abandoned that topic for now. He thought hard for a minute, and then he proceeded to fill Leon in on the events from the night before. The wound on his arm itched as he told his story.

"Somebody put a hit on you?" Leon exclaimed.

"Looks that way. And it didn't take long for them to find me. Leon, I need to know if you told *anybody* where I was staying."

"I ain't talked to nobody, dude. Don't plan on it, either."

"Maybe you bragged to a few of your buddies about hanging with the Widowmaker? You meant no harm, I'm sure."

"I ain't got no friends. Since Vonda left me, I ain't got nobody, man."

"Leon, do you know anyone who goes by the nickname 'Daddy?' "

"Can't say as I do."

"It was worth a shot." Nick reached into his jacket then. "I almost forgot. I've got something to give you."

"What's this?"

"It's a Trac-Fone. Picked one up for myself too. They're cheap pay-as-you-go deals, nothing fancy like the kids are using these days, but they'll work for our purposes. I thought it'd be a good idea for Melissa to be able to contact me any time she needs to. Figured it wouldn't hurt for the two of us to stay in touch as well."

"You bought me a *cellar* phone?" Leon said.

"Throw it out when I leave town, for all I care. But while I'm here, I need you to call me right away if you hear anything around town about Sophie, or if you see anybody snooping around Eddie's place."

"Dude, I don't have a clue how to use one of these contraptions."

"I spent all morning translating the user's manual, already got it programmed for you. All you have to do is answer it if it rings. It'll say 'WIDOWMAKER' on the little screen when I call."

That earned a grin from Leon. He held the phone up to his ear, inspected its shiny silver buttons. When he sat it down on the bar, though, he kept one eye on the phone, as if it were something that might jump up and latch onto his carotid artery if he dropped his guard for a second.

"Somebody tried to off you, man. I can't believe that shit!"

"It's true," said Nick.

"Say the dude had a silencer and everything? It's like somethin' outta one of them old private-eye flicks!"

"I guess." Nick's tone was sardonic, yet at the same time somber. "But real life isn't black-and-white. I'm no Philip Marlowe. And I'm surrounded by rejects from *Deliverance* instead of double-crossing dames with perfect gams and tits out to here."

Leon beamed at the mention of tits. He gave his hero two thumbs up, oblivious to the fact that he had been insulted.

†

Dinnertime found Nick and his daughter again sitting in a corner booth at Annie's Country Diner. But they didn't stay for long, after he told her what the man who tried to kill him had said about Sophie ("Oh, God," she cried, "I knew it! Some pervert's got her locked up like he *owns* her!"). Nick tossed a few dollars onto the table to pay for their untouched sodas, helped her stagger outside as the diner's patrons looked on.

All morning, a bruise-colored sky had hinted of a storm on the way. Seconds after they climbed into Nick's Bronco, the threat was realized. Lightning flashed and thunder boomed as if all the angels in Heaven were throwing down in some celestial brawl.

One minute the air was still, the next Nick could barely see the world outside through the sheets of pouring rain.

In the passenger seat beside him, Melissa stared out her window. Her shoulders trembled, but her sobs were muted beneath the rhythm of the Bronco's wipers thumping back and forth like long, skinny arms warding off the blows of a bully. Wormy rivulets of rainwater trickled down the glass in front of her face.

"Where are we going?" Nick started up the vehicle. "You wanna sit here and talk, or should we—"

"Just drive," she said. "Anywhere. I don't care."

He nodded, pulled away from the curb. Before they headed down Main Street, Nick saw where his daughter had been staring: on a telephone pole a few feet from the Bronco, a soggy flyer with Sophie's face on it had been all but destroyed by the storm. The fourteen-year-old's features appeared to be melting in the rain.

Nick felt a chill.

"Mind if I smoke?" Melissa asked him.

"Be my guest."

She lit up. Her cigarette quivered in her grip. She rolled down her window a half-inch or so, tapped ashes through the gap.

Neither of them said another word until they had traveled out of the town common, into the wooded outskirts of Midnight. When he noticed his daughter was shivering, Nick cranked up the Bronco's heater. Mostly it just blew out cool, dusty air that smelled like someone's basement.

Softly, he said, "Tell me about her."

The storm howled around them. At least a minute passed before Melissa replied.

"She's a wonderful young lady." She continued to stare out her rain-streaked window, alternately chewing at her fingernails and taking long drags off her cigarette as she spoke. "Nothing like me when I was her age, thank God. She's got a good head on her shoulders. Worries about her epilepsy, of course. Says she wants to be a writer when she grows up. She loves coffee ice cream, and those caramel candies with the white stuff in the middle. She spends a lot of time at the library, although it's usually so she can get on the Internet, mess around on Facebook. She used to beg me all the time to cook her favorite dish, lasagna..."

Melissa let out a little whimper, wiped at her eyes with the sleeve of her denim jacket. She shivered again as she turned to look at her father.

"She's a great kid. You would love her."

"I'm sure I would. I can tell she means the world to you."

"I wish they knew how much it hurts, when they talk about why they think Sophie was the one who killed Eddie. It tears my heart in two. That's why I didn't tell you about Sophie's phone call at first. I didn't want you to think about me the way *they* do. Everybody in this frigging town, they look at me like I'm one of those piece-of-shit moms who knew what was going on but I turned a blind eye to it. I could *never* be like that. I cared a lot about Eddie, but if I thought for a second he was putting his hands on Sophie, I would have killed him myself."

Nick said, "The good news is, Sheriff Mackey knows he was wrong now. He can start looking at this from a different angle."

"I tried to tell him all along. Didn't matter that they confiscated her diary, took every scrap of paper out of her bedroom—every note, every homework assignment, even the doodles in the margins of her textbooks— but they never found a shred of evidence suggesting that Sophie had been abused. It didn't matter, 'cause they had her phone call. Ever since she called me from that payphone, Sheriff Mackey's had his mind made up about how the whole thing went down."

"You can't blame him," said Nick. "Until we knew what Leon saw that night, it's all he had to go on."

"I know."

Nick eased to a stop at an intersection, looked both ways through the storm to make sure nothing was coming. Hoped for the best. He hooked a right onto Howard Street, which would soon turn into Route 30 leading out of Polk County. The road was slick beneath the Bronco's tires.

They passed the Snake River, which bisected the town of Midnight into two near-perfect halves. The river resembled not so much a body of water as a black swath of *nothingness* beyond the trees that lined its banks. It wasn't too far from here, Nick remembered, where his parents' farmhouse once stood. He didn't bother looking for it, though, as the property had been sold and his childhood home torn down many years ago.

"You know," Melissa said, tossing her cigarette out into the rain, "after Mom died, I thought about ending it all. Not that I would ever have the guts to do something like that—I'm a wuss when it comes to pain, and can't stand the sight of blood—but I don't think that's the *only* thing that kept me from doing it. Weird as it sounds, I think I knew deep down inside that I still had something important to live for. I think...I knew I was gonna come clean with Sophie. Eventually. And we'd build a life together."

Nick didn't say anything.

"I think part of it was *you*, too."

At that, Nick took his eyes off of the road long enough to glance over at his daughter. "What do you mean?"

"I think I knew you would be here. One day. That you would come back for me."

Shame devoured his soul. "I didn't even show up for your mama's funeral, sweetheart."

"No. No, but you called. You sent flowers."

That much was true. Thousands of dollars worth, he'd sent. They were delivered to the church that day by a fleet of black vans. Definitely *not* Nick's finest moment.

She said, "That's not my point anyway. What I'm trying to say is...I knew there would be a day when I would get to know you. I don't know how I knew. But I can't help thinking that I held on after the cancer took Mom 'cause *you* were still out there, somewhere. I still saw you once every few years, so I wasn't ready to write you off completely. I had a feeling you'd come back for me, one day. Maybe we wouldn't live happily ever after. I know that's not the way it happens in real life. But *eventually* everything might work out like it's supposed to. Maybe not perfect, but...better. It *had* to get better."

"It hasn't worked out like it's supposed to, though," Nick said, as much as it pained him to say it. His big right hand dropped from the steering wheel, engulfed her left hand. "Your daughter's been kidnapped. You'll be thirty in—three, four months? I'm not even sure—and I've learned more about you in the last *day* than I've known your whole life. You called me as a last resort, Melissa. And the truth of it is, I came because I had *nothing better to do*. That sounds cold-hearted, fucking despicable, but I don't want you giving me credit I haven't earned. We both know if *this* had never happened to me—" he turned his head from side to side, indicating his facial disfigurement "—I never would have answered that phone in the first place. I'd be on the other side of the world, and you...you'd be out of sight, out of mind. Just like every other time in your life when you needed a father."

Melissa jerked her hand from his as if she had touched something hot. She crossed her arms like a sullen child.

He pulled off of the highway now, onto the gravel lot of an abandoned apple-packing warehouse. Needles of rain stabbed at the Bronco harder than ever. The windshield looked as if it were covered with a wrinkled gray blanket. But Nick's reasons for pulling over went beyond poor visibility. He had something to say.

He jerked the gearshift into park. Turned to face his daughter.

"I'm not trying to hurt you, baby. That's the last thing I want to do. I'm just being honest. For once. I owe you that. I need to admit what I am. To you, and to myself. But that doesn't mean I can't *try* to be something better. I've never wanted anything more in my whole miserable life. I didn't know that until yesterday. But it's true."

"Daddy..."

"I've only been back for a day. I can't change thirty years, just like that. I know it will take time. But I promise I'll make this right. Any way I can..."

"Just find Sophie," she said. "Bring her home. That's all I want."

She unbuckled her seatbelt then, scooted over on the seat beside him.

He wrapped one massive arm around her, gazed out at the storm. "I'd give anything to change who I was back then. The guy who abandoned you and your mama...I hate that son-of-a-bitch."

"You don't have to—"

"No, I *hate* him, the selfish punk I was back then. I wish I could go back in time and beat the shit out of him."

In spite of herself, Melissa let out a giggle. "Would you put him in a choke hold?"

"Worse."

She smiled up at him now, and Nick loved it. Despite his daughter's nicotine-yellowed teeth, the crow's feet around her eyes that made her look ten years older than her true age...that smile was the most beautiful thing he had ever seen.

"I'd do my signature move on his ass," he said.

"Your big finish!"

"You remember it?"

They said it together then, in that ominous tone the announcers had used back when the Widowmaker was pro wrestling's most hated monster heel:

"...the FUNERAL MARCH!"

As if on cue, bright white lightning illuminated the world outside the Bronco. A crack of thunder vibrated through the vehicle's chassis, rattled its windows. The sound was like the world's largest two-by-four being split in two.

"I used to watch you on TV every Saturday morning," Melissa said. "Other kids loved their cartoons. I waited all week to see *GWA Mayhem*."

"I'm sure your mother didn't approve."

"She didn't. But I never missed it."

Nick chewed at the wrinkled fold of recycled skin where his bottom lip had once been. Awkwardly, he kissed the top of his daughter's head. She'd been six years old the last time he remembered doing that. This time her hair smelled like cigarette smoke.

She nestled in his arms, as if she had never been more comfortable. "You know what she used to say about you?"

"I'm sure she said a lot. Let me have it."

"No, it was nothing like that. Mom never badmouthed you. Not where I could hear."

That sounds just like Arlene, Nick thought. It was the kind of person she had been. No need to convince their impressionable young daughter that her father was a piece of shit—he had done a fine job of that on his own.

"She told me she never felt safer than she did when she was in your arms. She said when you two were in high school, you'd hold her, and all of her worries just melted away. She felt like you could protect her from anything."

Nick swallowed a lump in his throat, peered out into the rain.

"Didn't matter you were always the bad guy on TV. Growing up, I imagined you as this invincible giant. My guardian angel...or demon, I guess I should say."

"You sure had me wrong, didn't you?"

"You were my daddy. I was so proud of you, even if I barely knew you."

"Didn't bother you when your daddy rubbed ground glass in other dudes' eyes, rolled 'em up in barbed-wire as a sacrifice to Moloch? Some role model."

Melissa laughed. But then her brow furrowed. She leaned forward, squinted.

"Jeez...is that *hail*?"

Outside, the rain had tapered off, making way for an assault of ping-pong-ball-sized chunks of ice falling from the heavens. They bounced upon the gravel, rolled atop the asphalt, churned in foamy white drifts along the shoulder of the highway. They pinged, popped, and pounded violently on the Bronco's roof and hood.

The storm's roar grew to an almost deafening level. An image flashed through Nick's mind: twenty-thousand marks booing, hissing, stomping their feet and throwing things as the Widowmaker stalked down the entrance ramp...

And then it was gone. He returned to the here and now.

He held his daughter tightly. They were like two pieces of an unfinished puzzle, mismatched pieces that didn't quite fit together but they would have to suffice for now.

They sat like that for the next half hour or so, saying nothing more as the sky battered the earth relentlessly.

Dents stippled the Bronco's hood. An ugly crack appeared in the windshield, followed immediately by another: one on Melissa's side, one on Nick's. The cracks grew larger, stretching across the glass until they met in the middle.

It might have been the End of the World out there.

But as he held his daughter in his arms, Nick Bullman was content for the first time in years.

He came in from the storm, dripping all over the motel's main office like an old mutt.

If the woman behind the front desk wasn't the most obese human being he had ever seen, she came in a close second. Straight brown hair that looked like it hadn't been washed in weeks fell to her ample belly. Atop her upper lip, she sported nearly a full moustache. Her massive breasts sagged beneath a wrinkled Appalachian State University sweatshirt.

As Nick approached the front desk, she didn't look up from the *Cosmopolitan* she was reading.

"Ma'am, I don't suppose you have an Internet connection in this fine establishment?" he asked her.

"We do," she replied, still not looking up from her magazine. "Free for guests to use."

"Would you mind showing me the way to the business center?"

"Ain't got one of those. Just a 'puter. Around the corner, by the payphones."

"Thanks." Nick did a little fingertip drum-roll on the countertop. "I'll let you get back to your magazine."

He found what he was looking for in a small alcove at the rear of the building. He unzipped his jacket, removed his wet wool cap. Adjusted the swivel chair in front of the desk to a tolerable level of uncomfortability. Bold black letters typed on a strip of paper taped to the monitor warned: TIME LIMIT 10 MIN IF OTHER GUEST ARE WAITING!!!!! Someone had drawn a penis on the note in red marker. Nick wondered how often folks lined up waiting for their turn at the computer in a joint like this.

He had never been an avid Internet user, but he could find his way around cyberspace if his life depended on it. Several years ago, he had worked with a young fan—a nephew of a friend in the Biz—who had offered to build for him an official Widowmaker website. In the process, he had learned how to send and receive e-mail (although he could count on one hand the times he had used it since) along with the basics of surfing the 'Net.

That experience would come in handy now, he hoped. The idea had struck him as he made his way back into town, after he'd dropped Melissa off at her apartment. He thought it might be worth his time to do some more research on Eddie Whiteside's scuffles with the law. Probably wouldn't hurt to try digging up some info on other key players in this case as well. At this point he would take anything he could get.

Nick hunched over the computer. The room was silent save for the machine's low hum and the murmur of rain on the roof overhead.

He opened a browser, brought up Google, typed "MIDNIGHT SUN" and "POLK COUNTY, NC" into the search field. Took him several tries to get it right; his fingers were like kielbasa sausages hunting-and-pounding on the tiny keyboard.

Before long, though, he found what he was looking for: the official website of his hometown's newspaper, the *Midnight Sun*.

He typed Eddie's name into a field labeled SEARCH ARCHIVES. This led him to a brief article that told him nothing he didn't already know. Earlier this year, Eddie had been arrested during a routine traffic stop after the police found "small quantities of marijuana and drug paraphernalia" in his truck. He was charged with misdemeanor possession, and the authorities subsequently obtained a warrant to search his home on Gorman Gap Road. The article mentioned that "others living in the residence" were questioned, but no further charges were filed.

A dark suspicion nibbled at the back of Nick's brain. Something about that search of Eddie's house, and the fact that the cops came away empty-handed...

It didn't add up. Shouldn't they have found *something*? Eddie was a dealer.

Nick searched for Melissa's name next. He wasn't sure why, and he felt more than a little guilty about it, but after a quick glance over his shoulder he did it anyway.

There were no results prior to the date Sophie went missing.

Thunder rumbled outside. The lights flickered.

Nick was ready to head back to his room now and admit to himself that this had been a waste of time. But then he remembered something Melissa had mentioned earlier, about how Sophie spent a lot of time on Facebook. Although he wasn't entirely sure what a Facebook was, he searched for it next along with Sophie's name. He wanted to learn more about his granddaughter, wished to see Sophie from *her* point of view, and maybe this would help...

Perhaps he'd even get lucky, discover that she had updated her Facebook whatchamathing in the days since she went missing. He was pretty sure the police had ways of pinpointing her location, if that were the case. Then again, they had probably thought of that already.

He realized that he could go no further without being a member of the site himself, so he took a minute to register, using the name "John Smith." Once that was done, finding her was effortless. There were seventeen Facebook users who shared the same first and last name as his granddaughter, but the first "Sophie Suttles" on the list of results was accompanied by a photo of a young lady Nick recognized even though he had never met her in person. Her location, still listed as "Hickory, NC," helped narrow his search as well. She was blowing the camera a kiss in her profile picture.

She had last logged on the day before she went missing.

Nick slowly scrolled down the page.

She had eighty-seven Facebook "Friends." Most of them were local girls her own age, kids Nick assumed she knew from school. Numerous comments had been left by her buddies on her Wall, but lighthearted greetings like "GOING 2 THE MOVIES FRIDAY NITE?," "THX 4 THE BDAY CARD SOPH," and "DEVIN WALKER SEZ YOUR CUTE – TOLD U SO!!!" had been replaced within the last thirty days by darker lamentations such as "WE MISS U," "PRAYING 4 YOUR SAFE RETURN," and "POLK CTY COPS DONT KNOW THERE ASSES FROM A HOLE IN TEH GROUND: FIND SOPHIE SUTTLES!!!!!1!"

There was nothing much to see beyond that, though a list of questions-and-answers on the "Notes" section of her page caught Nick's eye...

More than ever, he yearned to meet this young lady. He only hoped this silly Internet questionnaire wasn't the most he would *ever* know about her:

*** LUCKY 13: 13 QUESTIONS, ALL ABOUT MOI ***

#1) WHAT'S YOUR BEST FRIEND'S NAME?
MOM

#2) WHAT COLOR UNDERWEAR ARE YOU WEARING?
NOYB

#3) RIGHT NOW I'M LISTENING TO:

the rain outside my window

#4) WHAT'S THE LAST THING YOU ATE?

lasagna

#5) FAVORITE HOLIDAY:

Christmas

#6) THE LAST MOVIE I WATCHED:

don't remember, some cheesy horror movie

#7) WHAT BOOK YOU ARE CURRENTLY READING?

The Scarlet Letter (for school but it's actually pretty kewl)

#8) HAVE YOU EVER LOVED SOMEONE?

not like that

#9) EVER FIRED A GUN?

yep (last weekend was my first time, my mom's boyfriend bought me a tattoo & taught me how to shoot all in the same day—it was BAD-ASS!!!!!!!!!!)

#10) SMOKE/DRINK/DO DRUGS?

gross/no/does my epilepsy medicine count? <g>

#11) DO YOU HAVE A TEMPER?

not really

#12) THE CELEBRITY I WOULD MOST LIKE TO MEET ONE DAY:

an old wrestler named the Widowmaker (he's my grandfather—no joke!)

#13) HOW DO YOU WANT TO BE REMEMBERED WHEN

that I treated people good

The words on the screen blurred. Nick plucked his trusty handkerchief from his back pocket and wiped his eyes with it, hard.

The celebrity I would most like to meet one day: An old wrestler named the Widowmaker. He's my grandfather...

For once, it wasn't just Nick's right eye that leaked uncontrollably now.

Before he closed the computer's browser and retired to his room, he reread #9. At least a dozen times.

His heart raced as he tried to make sense of it.

Have you ever fired a gun?

Sophie's reply: *Last weekend was my first time...my mom's boyfriend taught me how to shoot...*

✝

The next morning he sat in his motel room, munching on a hard sausage biscuit from the Gas-N-Go across the street while he thumbed through the *Midnight Sun*. On the paper's front page was an article recapping Eddie Whiteside's murder exactly one month ago, and the subsequent search for Sophie Suttles. A piece further down the page detailed the events at the Sunrise Motor Lodge ("SHOOTER STILL UNIDENTIFIED"), and while the writer of this article hinted that what happened there might have some connection to Sophie's disappearance, Sheriff Mackey and his men had declined to corroborate, so the focus was more on the fact that Nick Bullman was a former TV celebrity born here in Polk County than on his blood relation to the missing teen.

Nick tossed the newspaper onto his bedside table, reached for the remote control to turn up *Good Morning America*. One of his old cohorts had written a "tell-all" autobiography about his life in the Biz, his struggles with sex addiction and steroid abuse, and now he was coming on the show to talk about how Lance K. McDougal III had bribed his publisher into burying the book. Needless to say, Nick was intrigued.

But when the phone rang he almost dropped his biscuit.

He brushed crumbs from his lap, muted the television before picking up the receiver.

"Yeah? Who is it?"

"Mr. Bullman? Sheriff Mackey."

"Sheriff."

"I wish I was calling with better news. Thought you'd like to know that we got the results back on your man's fingerprints. Came up with jack shit. No criminal record. Nor has ever served in the military."

"Dammit," said Nick.

"No luck with his gun, either. The serial numbers had been filed off. That doesn't always work as well as most folks think, but in this case we got nothing."

"So what happens now?"

"I want to talk with the owner of the motel again. Hopefully something will jog his memory."

"Wouldn't hold my breath if I were you," Nick grunted.

Papers rustled on the sheriff's end of the line. A police scanner beeped and squawked. "In the meantime," said Mackey, "an associate of mine is working up a sketch of our John Doe. I aim to get that on the front page of the *Sun* by this weekend. Somebody's seen this guy around—just a first name would be a hell of a start—chances are it'll lead to a known accomplice or two."

"I appreciate the update, Sheriff," said Nick.

"Don't thank me, Mr. Bullman. It's my job. Contrary to what you might think, we are on the same side here."

"Never said we weren't."

"I know this is hard for you. Hard for your daughter. About what I said the other night...hell, I've known Melissa since she was in middle school."

"She told me that."

"Well, I guess that's all for now. I'll be in touch."

Nick hung up the phone.

✝

Around noon Nick pocketed his keys, preparing to go out. Exactly *where* he was headed he hadn't decided yet. At some point he planned to revisit the house on Gorman Gap Road, since his initial search of the place had been rudely interrupted. Also, he thought he might spend a day or two driving through a few of Midnight's neighboring towns and cities (Hendersonville, Columbus, Tryon, Morganville); maybe he'd get lucky, spot Sophie hanging out near the homeless shelters or on a park bench somewhere. It was an extremely long shot, but it was better than nothing.

He felt restless. Had to get out and do *something*. Sophie wasn't going to just fall out of the sky, land in his lap, and they'd all live happily ever after. It was time to *move...*

But then, as he was preparing to do exactly that, Nick heard a knock at the door of his motel room.

It was quiet, tentative. Although he doubted anyone would come gunning for him in broad daylight, he hefted the tire iron he had brought in from the Bronco, carried it across the room with him.

He nudged aside the curtain. Then quickly unlocked the door and drew back the chain. "Melissa? Hey..."

The nasty weather from the night before had moved on, yet the day was still gray and damp, as if the storm had left its smaller brother behind to bully Midnight some more. A mist of light summer rain blew across the parking lot. Tires hissed on the nearby highway like conspiratorial whispers. At the corner of the building, a mangy stray dog cocked one leg and pissed on the side of a dumpster. From another open doorway a few rooms down, a woman bellowed over a too-loud TV that if she had to tell Toby one more time to pick his colorin' books offa the floor he'd be sorry.

Behind Melissa, in the parking spot directly in front of Nick's room, her Toyota idled quietly. Nick saw what looked like several bulky grocery bags sitting in the passenger seat.

His daughter took one last drag off her cigarette, tossed the butt out in the rain before she spoke.

"Can I come in?"

"Of course." He stepped aside. "Is everything okay?"

She rushed past him, plopped down on the edge of the bed. "It's been one month today."

"I know."

She started chewing at her fingernails, as if that was what she had come here to do.

"You, uh, wanna turn off your car, stay a while?" Nick asked her.

"I can't. I have to drop by work, pick up my paycheck. I just wanted to come by and..."

He eased the door shut, then quickly moved to sit beside her. Beneath his added weight, the bed sank all the way to the floor.

"What is it, Melissa? What's going on?"

"I wanted to ask you something. I didn't call 'cause I wanted to ask you in person."

"I'm listening."

"This is gonna sound crazy, with everything else going on. And you gotta understand...it's not that Sophie isn't on my mind every second of every day. God knows she is. But I need to stay *sane*. I need to have some sort of...routine. For both of us. And I think something like this...it'll go a long way toward helping me feel like I'm keeping things *normal* for her...for when Sophie comes home."

"I'm sorry," Nick said. "I'm not sure what you're asking me to—"

"I want to cook dinner for you," she said. "Will you come to my apartment? Tonight? Will you let me make Sophie's favorite dish for you?"

"Lasagna," he remembered.

She gave him a sad little smile.

"Melissa, you don't owe me anything—"

"I know. That's not why I'm doing this. I just...it's what I *need*, okay?"

I want someone to enjoy Sophie's favorite meal the way she used to. She begged me to make it several times a week. Eddie got so he couldn't stand the smell of it. Now that she's gone, I'd give anything to bake my lasagna for her again. To hear her say how much she loved it."

"Well, then," said Nick, "I would love to try your lasagna, if you're sure you're up to it."

"I've already bought the stuff to make it," she said. "Just got back from the grocery store."

"Great. I'll be there."

"How does six o'clock sound?"

"It's a date."

She told him how to get to her new apartment. They said their goodbyes for now, and she hurried outside to her car.

Nick watched his daughter's Camry depart through the drizzle.

He stood there in the doorway for several minutes after she was gone, lost in his thoughts. He barely even noticed the fate of that dog he'd seen pissing on the dumpster a few minutes ago; it lay mashed against the curb on the other side of the street now, flattened by a passing vehicle.

Elsewhere in the motel, that loud-mouthed mother was hollering at Toby to bring her a damn belt 'cause she was tired of talkin'.

Nick shook his head, closed the door.

He realized he was still holding the tire iron. Had been the whole time.

✝

He dropped his empty beer bottle into the wastebasket, where it clanked loudly against the three down in there that he had already drained.

He had dressed as nicely as he knew how for this occasion: blue silk shirt with black flames climbing up the torso, brown trousers, and snakeskin boots. But the shirt was too small for him; its buttons threatened to pop off and fly across the room with every breath he took. He hadn't realized the pants were so wrinkled until he was driving over here. As for the boots, he had owned them since Melissa was a toddler.

He was sure he looked ridiculous. Like pinning a diamond brooch on a warthog. Splashing cologne on a catfish. But as soon as his daughter answered the door, she had stood on her tiptoes, kissed him on one scar-hardened cheek. She told him he looked nice. And nothing else in this mean old world mattered.

"Smells delicious," he said now. "Anything I can do to help out in here?"

She was busy making a salad, slicing a plump tomato with a butcher knife. "Nope. Just stay out of my way."

"Far be it from me to argue with a woman wielding a blade."

He watched her finish with the tomato, whirl to check on her lasagna in the oven, then pause to light a cigarette. Her eyes were once again red, swollen, as if she had spent most of her day crying, but he could tell she was happy to have him here. She wanted this evening to be perfect.

"Hope you're hungry." Her cigarette bounced between her lips as she whittled away at a carrot.

Truthfully, Nick didn't have much of an appetite. The aromas that filled her kitchen smelled heavenly, no doubt about it, but a hard ball of anxiety had settled in his stomach since he first entered her apartment. He feared they were wasting precious time—standing here bullshitting, preparing a hearty feast, while his granddaughter was out there somewhere, undoubtedly terrified and being forced to do God-knew-what. But Melissa had explained to him why she needed to do this. If this was what it took to dry her tears for a few hours, to help give her some semblance of peace until Sophie was found, so be it.

He left her alone in the kitchen, wandered into the living room.

Melissa's place was sparsely furnished, devoid of anything that might have given it any sense of *her*. The spartan furniture and dimestore decor had obviously been provided by her landlord. No pictures hung on the apartment's cream-colored walls. The only exception was a framed photo of Sophie in one corner of the living room; it sat on a crooked end-table next to a portable CD player. A potted plant with ragged brown leaves occupied one windowsill like a tormented soul contemplating suicide. The view from that second-story window: railroad tracks, a coin laundry, and a seedy-looking pool hall.

Nick paced back and forth across the living room, his hands in his pockets. Through the apartment's thin walls, he heard a toilet flush. Bass-heavy Latino music thumped from the speakers of a passing car down on the street.

He felt more restless than ever.

He wandered over to the CD player, saw a single shiny jewelcase beside it: *The Very Best of Etta James*. He pushed PLAY.

Etta sang her heart out about how she wished someone would care.

A *ding* from the kitchen then. Silverware rattled in an opened drawer, and Melissa called out to him with an update: five more minutes, and it'd be time for dinner.

"I'll wash up," said Nick.

"Bathroom's at the end of the hall," she said. "You'll have to let the water run for a minute. It always comes out rusty at first. Looks like blood."

✝

He finished washing his hands, drying them, and now he found himself just standing there, staring into the mirror above the sink.

The face that leered back at him was like something out of a horror flick. A mad scientist's creation dressed up in the best Midnight Big & Tall had to offer.

Nick took a deep breath, let it out slowly. Otherwise, he didn't move. He just stood there. Not even blinking. Staring at his own wretched face...

...something he hadn't done for the better part of a year-and-a-half.

Not that he'd been counting the days. He just knew. The way other folks could recall how long it had been since they took a trip to the beach, made love, or confessed their sins to a priest.

The last time Nick Bullman had intentionally looked in a mirror, he'd been sitting up in a hospital bed in Durham, North Carolina. He was hooked up to IVs that pumped him full of painkillers every time he tapped the little joystick the nurses had placed in his palm (which he did, frequently; it probably looked as if he were playing a videogame no one else could see). The doctors had done the best they could. But he knew he wasn't the only one who felt a sense of crushing disappointment when the bandages came off. As the fidgety young nurse held a mirror up to his face, they informed him that there had been extensive nerve damage. The men who attacked him had sliced deeply into muscle, even nicking bone with their blade. Infection had set in. He nearly lost one eye. Things might have turned out differently if they'd had his real face to work with. If someone had thought to pick it up off the floor that night, put it on ice, they might have been able to reattach it. Unfortunately, the face Nick Bullman was born with had been "regrettably misplaced," according to the official euphemism (he imagined some hick cop confusing it for a wad of bloody rags, sweeping it into a dustpan and tossing it out with the trash). He listened to their spiel, saying nothing, trying not to hate them despite the fact that, mere minutes before they walked into his room, he awoke sweat-drenched and screaming from a surreal Dilaudid dream…a nightmare in which a gang of prankster surgeons grafted stiff pink nipples, wrinkled scrotum skin, and puckered brown anuses all over his new "face."

As he lay there gazing with a sick stomach upon the mess that had become of his once-handsome features, he squeezed the handle of the nurse's makeup mirror so tightly it broke off in his hand.

At that moment Nick vowed never to look into a mirror again.

Mirrors were hateful inventions. They existed only to torment him. He loathed them like most folks loath speeding tickets, head lice, and waiting in really long lines.

Of course, it would have been silly to suggest that he had gone a whole year-and-a-half without glancing into a reflective surface even *once*. Naturally, he caught glimpses of himself out of the corner of his eye: in his Bronco's cracked rearview mirror, in the lenses of a stranger's sunglasses, in the gray square of a television screen seconds before he turned it on.

One thing he made sure of, though: he *never* did it on purpose.

But so much had changed these last few days.

Nick knew he had never been a "good person." Since returning to his hometown, though, he felt as if a great weight had lifted off of his shoulders. He was starting to think he *could* be, one day. Something akin to a "good person."

Nick Bullman didn't know shit about self-analysis. But he did know he was *trying*. And that had to stand for something, didn't it, in the grand scheme of things?

At last, he had confronted his inner fiend. He decided it was long past time that he gazed upon the grotesque *outside* of himself as well.

You wanna reveal a man's true colors, sometimes you gotta dig deep, get to the skull beneath the skin...

It had taken a combination of over two thousand stitches and staples to fix him up. A total of six operations over a period of eight grueling months. Numerous skin grafts from his thighs, back, and buttocks...

This was what he had to show for it all.

Dear God, it was so much worse than he ever thought.

But he might have finally learned to live with it. Since he had found something worth living *for*.

✝

"Dad? You okay in there?"

A rap at the bathroom door. Nick flinched, knocked over a bottle of liquid soap. It clattered into the sink with one of Melissa's toothbrushes.

"Uh, yeah," he said, putting everything back where it belonged. "I'll be right there. Sorry."

"I was worried you might have fallen in." Melissa's voice was muffled through the bathroom door.

Nick took a moment to compose himself.

"Dinner's waiting, whenever you're ready. Um...are you sure everything's okay?"

He turned his back on the mirror at last, quickly opened the door. As if their roles were reversed: Melissa was the parent, he was her child, and she had caught him doing something naughty. He stepped out into the hallway, wrapped his huge arms around her.

She had been drying her hands on a dishtowel prior to his embrace. When he released her, she said, "What was that for?"

"Nothing." He wiped a smear of pasta sauce from her cheek, licked it off his thumb. "Let's eat."

The apartment's dining area consisted of an old cherrywood table sitting in one corner of the living room. The table's surface was scarred with deep gouges that suggested an axe murderer might have used it for practice at some point.

Melissa apologized as she and her father sat.

"This is wonderful," said Nick. "Don't be sorry."

He noticed she had set a third place at the head of the table: silverware, a salad bowl, a dish with a small helping of lasagna in the center. As if for a guest-of-honor who had not yet arrived.

She caught him looking at the empty chair. "It's silly, I know."

"Not at all," he said.

"It's something I have to do. I always make a plate for her. Even though I end up throwing it out when I'm done. But I can't help it. I refuse to think of her in the past tense, you know? I won't. 'Cause that would be giving up."

"I understand."

She sat there for a few more seconds, staring at Sophie's plate.

Finally, she snapped out of it. She picked up her fork, nodded toward the mound of lasagna in front of him. "Dig in."

Nick did. And after only several bites he decided that he had never eaten anything more delicious. He knew now why Sophie couldn't get enough of her mother's lasagna, why she had asked for it night after night. The kid had great taste.

Nick watched Melissa pick at her salad, sip at her bottle of beer. Every so often she moved her lasagna around on her plate. Mostly, though, she just drank beer.

For the next several minutes they ate in silence, save for Etta James in the background, the clinking of forks on dishware, and Nick's satisfied crunching/smacking (he tried his best to control it, but with no lips this was a feat easier said than done).

"Well?" Melissa said. "I'm assuming you like it?"

"*Like* it? This is fantastic, hon."

She glanced toward the untouched plate at the head of the table again, looked like she was about to say something else, but then returned her attention to her own meal.

Outside the apartment's single window, the day slowly died. A train passed on the tracks below.

About the time he set his silverware down, belched into one fist and rested his elbows on the tabletop, Melissa spoke again. As if she'd been thinking about this all along and decided she'd better say what was on her mind while she had the chance.

"Did you know I came to see you while you were in the hospital?"

Nick was stunned. "What?"

"I came to see you. Twice, actually. The first time was right after I heard about what those men did to you. I was at work. I saw the news on the TV above the bar. I borrowed some money from my boss that night, took the red-eye down to Amarillo."

Nick said, "Oh, baby..."

"The second time, you were at Duke. It was after one of your surgeries."

"I had no idea. I never knew—"

"Both times you were fast asleep. I didn't stay long. I asked them not to tell you that I came. I don't know why."

Nick's dinner sat heavy in his stomach, like a pile of soggy mulch. He hung his head, ran one hand over his prickly gray buzzcut. "I can't believe you *cared*."

Melissa reached across the table to touch her father's hand. "You look like you could use another beer."

"Or ten," he said.

She laughed. As she headed for the kitchen, she called over her shoulder, "I'll bring the whole case, how's that? I might even help you finish it off."

"You're a big girl. I won't try to stop you."

On the CD player, Etta James crooned: *"Cling to me, Daddy, and I'll be strong...we'll get along..."*

The song couldn't have been more appropriate. Nick felt a bone-deep chill.

He wondered if Melissa felt it too.

†

His brain felt like it was slamming against the inside of his skull with every beat of his heart. At first, opening his eyes was pure agony, thanks to a beam of bright morning sunlight that stabbed through a gap in the curtains, spotlighting him square in the face.

A foul taste filled his mouth, coated the back of his throat. This conjured mental images of another intruder breaking into his room in the middle of the night...this time, however, the culprit was interested not in killing Nick Bullman, but making him the victim of a vile prank. 'Cause damned if it didn't taste like someone had squatted over him while he slept, taken a big greasy dump down his gullet.

Nick swallowed, winced. Rubbed at his throbbing temples.

"Christ Almighty..."

The way he felt this morning, he might have been out on the road again, just ten or twelve hours after a Last Man Standing match with some stiff worker like Chris "The Cannibal" Cartman or Vesuvius.

"Idiot. Guy your age ought to know better."

He couldn't remember the last time he'd been hungover.

After they had called it a night at Melissa's place, he had driven back to his motel room sporting a considerable buzz. While he hadn't been anywhere close to shitfaced, there was no doubt in Nick's mind that he would have woken up this morning wearing an orange jumpsuit, size 4X, if Polk County's Finest had pulled him over. This brought to mind the tragedy that had befallen a friend of his several years ago. A star-on-the-rise named William Denny—"Billy All-American" in the ring—had gone out to a bar one night after his divorce was finalized and drank himself into oblivion. On his way home, Denny's Charger had crossed over the median and struck a minivan head-on. For the rest of his life, he had to live with the fact that he had killed a woman and her eight-year-old daughter. Nick shuddered as he remembered his friend—a grown man who could bench-press twice his own body weight—bawling like a baby from behind bars. He remembered how Billy All-American had once ranked among the most beloved "babyfaces" in the Biz...but now the marks' red-white-and-blue-clad hero might never have existed at all. His was a name no longer mentioned by the Global Wrestling Association, lest it tarnish the brand's reputation.

Nick forced his mind back to the present, shook his head in self-disgust. "Could've been you, asshole..."

As for Melissa, she'd gotten so drunk she passed out on her sofa. Nick figured it had been a long time coming, with everything on her mind these last few weeks; he couldn't begrudge her this one night of drowning her problems with alcohol. Before he left her apartment, he had covered her with an old wool blanket draped over the back of the couch. He sat there staring at his daughter for ten or fifteen minutes before finally staggering outside to his Bronco.

Now he shook his head again, swung his legs over the side of the bed. He wiped crusty sleep-stuff from the corner of his right eye. Shot a glance at the clock on the nightstand: 8:48 a.m.

The phone rang.

The sound was like shards of broken glass stabbing through his eardrums, digging through the meat of his brain.

He reached over, knocked the phone off its cradle. Stifling a burp that threatened to turn into something worse, he bent to retrieve the dangling receiver.

"What is it?" he growled into the phone.

"Mr. Bullman? 'Morning."

"Sheriff."

"I'm calling to tell you that it looks like we might finally have a lead."

Nick stood, too quickly. He swayed on his feet.

"Last night around one a.m.," Mackey said, "a drugstore about nine miles from here was broken into. A small, family-owned place called Boden & Sons, in Tryon."

Nick paced back and forth. The phone's cord stretched tight between the receiver in his hand and its cradle on the nightstand.

"He came in through the back. Busted out a window. He knew exactly what he was looking for, never even touched the register."

The sheriff didn't have to tell Nick what the burglar had been after. The big man knew. Instantly. It was an act of desperation, this robbery. But it wasn't one of those drugstore smash-and-grabs you read about in the papers—some punk looking to score a few bottles of Oxycontin or Xanax. He remembered what Melissa had told him that day at the diner, about how her daughter suffered from epilepsy, and the medication Sophie took to keep her seizures at bay...

"Lamictal."

"Got it in one," said the sheriff. "Son-of-a-bitch cleaned out their entire supply."

Who are *these people?* Nick wondered. *They obviously don't mind* killing *to achieve their goals...so why do they appear to be taking such good* care *of Sophie? What do they want her for?*

Every possible answer to those questions made Nick feel like vomiting. And not because of his hangover. He covered his mouth with a fist.

"Here's where it gets good," said the sheriff. "The store has a single security camera, above the register. It's wired into a computer in an office in the back. After hours, the camera is set to record only when it detects movement."

"I'll be damned," said Nick. "You got him on video."

"I'm telling you he practically *posed* for us."

"I'll be damned," Nick said again.

"There is, uh, one more thing."

"Shoot."

"It's gonna sound crazy. But I saw it with my own two eyes."

Mackey hesitated.

"Mr. Bullman...if I didn't know better, I'd think the man on that video was the same man who tried to kill you at the Sunrise Motor Lodge. The man we both watched get *zipped up in a body bag*, and loaded into the back of that ambulance."

†

"Holy shit! Yeah, I've seen him. I *have* seen that dude!"

Leon had been slouching in a chair in one corner of Nick's room, his yellow moped helmet in his lap. But suddenly he sat up straight, as if an electric current had shot through his lanky frame. The helmet tumbled onto the floor.

"That's him alright. Sure as I'm sittin' here."

Several hours after their morning chat, Sheriff Mackey had called Nick again, this time to inform him that the video footage recorded at Boden & Sons' Pharmacy would be airing on Channel 13's *News At 6*. Nick had dialed up Leon right away, insisting that he watch the broadcast; maybe he would recognize the man from the drugstore. Of course, Nick wasn't surprised to learn that Leon had pawned his own TV a while back. So he told him to come to the MountainView Motel, and they would watch the news together.

"Don't be late," he had strongly suggested.

Leon obliged, puttering up on his moped a few minutes before six p.m. He wore acid-washed jeans and a T-shirt from a band called Your Kid's On Fire.

As the eight-second clip was replayed, a pretty young reporter explained what had happened at Boden & Sons' Pharmacy in Tryon the night before. While specific details regarding what was stolen had not yet been disclosed, she said, local authorities were asking citizens for help identifying this man who might be connected to the disappearance of

Sophie Lynn Suttles. At this point an image of the missing teen—the same photo Nick carried in his Bronco—flashed across the screen, but Sophie's face was there and gone so fast it was barely more than a subliminal suggestion.

The reporter rattled off the phone number for the Tryon Police Department before the video was shown one last time. Halfway through, the clip froze, giving viewers a final look at the drugstore burglar.

Nick and Leon rose from their seats, and stood together in front of the TV like two men captivated by a nail-biting turn of events in some live sports spectacle.

The man on the screen was hefting a crowbar above his head, preparing to destroy the camera. He was a short, stocky man with a receding hairline, a salt-and-pepper goatee. The store's cash register was visible behind him, and beyond that tall white shelves stocked with hundreds of pill bottles. A black duffel bag sat beside the register, unzipped and empty but waiting to be filled.

Nick couldn't believe his eyes. Sheriff Mackey hadn't lost his mind after all.

The man in the video looked *exactly* like the man who had broken into his room at the Sunrise Motor Lodge...a thug who now lay in the Polk County Morgue with a hole in his throat.

He was even wearing the same clothes he had worn the night he tried to kill Nick in his sleep: Dark suit. Western-style bolo tie. The only difference Nick could see was his demeanor, if one could judge such a thing from a single image. Where the gunman at the motel had never raised his voice, had in fact seemed almost *kind* at first (the fact that he had been trying to murder Nick notwithstanding), his doppelganger appeared full of rage in the footage captured by the drugstore camera. His teeth were bared, his eyes wild. His forehead glistened with sweat.

"Who is this son-of-a-bitch, Leon? Where can I find him?"

"Can't help you with his name," said Leon, "but I've seen him around for sure. He hangs out sometimes at the Skin Den."

"What the hell's a *skindin*?"

"It don't really have a name. Everybody just calls it that. The Skin Den. It's a titty bar off Highway 64, just this side of Morganville."

"Tell me about him. Tell me everything you know."

"Not a lot to tell. Once in a blue moon, if I've got a few bucks to burn or I can con some other fool into buyin', I'll drop by the 'Den for a shot or two. Slide some dollar bills in some thongs, watch some asses shake." Leon gestured toward the TV, but by now the pretty reporter had moved on to a piece about a dog show at the Asheville Civic Center this weekend. "Every now and then, this dude shows up."

"How often?"

"I don't know."

"Dammit, *think*, Leon."

"It ain't like I hang out there all the time myself. Maybe once every couple o' months. I've seen him about every other time I've been in there."

"Is he a popular guy? Big spender?"

Leon shrugged. "He usually just sits at the same table in the corner. Keeps to himself."

"Have you ever talked to him?"

"Nobody says much to anybody in a place like the 'Den. They're either lookin' down at their beer or starin' up at titties. Usually the titties."

Nick was desperate to learn more. He wanted to grab Leon, shake more info out of him. At last, a potential path to Sophie had presented itself. It was vague, obscured by the swirling fog of so many unknown factors, but it was there.

"What about Eddie? Did he hang out at this *Skin Den*?"

"Sometimes."

"Ever see him talking to the guy in the video?"

"Now that you mention it, I think I did," Leon said. "Hey! You asked me before who Eddie worked for. You reckon this guy mighta been his supplier? Maybe with Eddie gone, he's hurtin' for cash, and he's plannin' to sell whatever he stole from the drugstore!"

"No," said Nick. "There's more to this than what's right in front of our faces. This thing goes deeper than Eddie playing truck-stop pimp, selling dime bags to you and your buddies."

Nick turned off the TV then, took a few minutes to fill Leon in on all of the details not provided by the news program: how the drugstore robbery was connected to Sophie, and how the man who had absconded with the pharmacy's entire supply of Lamictal appeared to be the same man who had tried to murder him.

Leon listened, grinding his teeth the whole time. His eyes were huge and alien-like behind his Coke-bottle glasses.

"Are you thinkin' what I'm thinkin', hoss?" he said when Nick was done.

"Depends. What are you thinking?"

"Maybe this dude's some kinda *ghost*?"

Nick didn't dignify that with a response. Since speaking with the sheriff, he had decided on a more logical explanation: identical *twins*. But it was uncanny nonetheless, seeing that face on his TV screen...the face of a man whose violent death he had witnessed less than seventy-two hours ago.

Abruptly, he turned and scooped his keys off of the nightstand.

"Whatcha doin'?" Leon asked him.

"Going for a drive. And you're coming with me. How far is the club from here?"

"Hit the interstate, you could be there in twenty minutes. Is there any particular reason I have to tag along?"

"You know this joint, Leon. I'm going crazy just sitting here. My granddaughter needs me. I've got to *do* something."

"There's Bingo at the VFW every Friday night," Leon suggested.

"You know what I mean. Come on. I'll buy you a beer."

Leon's bony shoulders slumped, and as he followed Nick to the door he mumbled, "I'm tellin' you, dude...before all this is over, you're gonna get me killed."

"Look at the bright side. At least you'll die happy, get to stick your face between some double-Ds before we throw you in the ground."

"There is that," Leon said.

†

Nick made a quick detour across town first.

"Sit tight." He left the engine running. "This will only take a minute."

Leon sank down in his seat, gave his idol a sarcastic salute.

Nick knew it was a long shot, but he had driven to the Polk County Sheriff's Department hoping that Sheriff Mackey might supply him with a hard copy of the video capture shown on the news. Better than walking into the club empty-handed, asking if anyone had seen a stocky middle-aged dude with thinning salt-and-pepper hair. That undoubtedly described ninety percent of the Skin Den's clientele on any given night.

The station was quiet, the building empty save for three lonely souls. A Latino woman pushed a mop around the foyer while her little boy hunched over a handheld videogame. Sheriff Mackey sat behind his desk, nursing a headache with a bottle of Tylenol and a can of Diet Coke.

When Nick told the sheriff that he hadn't expected to find him so easily, Mackey said, "I've forgotten what home looks like. Probably why I've been through two divorces, working on my third as we speak." He tore a low-quality reproduction of the freeze-frame from the drugstore video—the scowling burglar in his fancy suit, gripping a crowbar in one hand—off of a cluttered corkboard. He made two copies on the department's Xerox machine, handed them over without pressing Nick too hard about why he wanted the photo. It was obvious Mackey had a million other things on his mind. And perhaps he had decided that he would take all the help he could get, at this point.

Twenty minutes later, the big man's Bronco rattled and quaked as it cruised down the interstate. The sky had taken on a surreal orange hue with the coming of dusk, as if the region and all of its inhabitants were prehistoric bugs stuck in an enormous block of amber. On the Bronco's stereo, Sunnyland Slim sang "The Devil Is a Busy Man."

Beside Nick, Leon stared out his window like a misbehaved student on his way to a visit with the principal. Every so often he tapped two fingers on his jittery knee in time with the music.

"Nervous?" Nick asked him.

"That's one word for it," said Leon. "Another way to put it is I'm scared to fuckin' death."

"I'd bet this is the first time anyone's had to twist Leon Purdy's arm to get him out to the strip club."

"Never went to one lookin' for a dude who's supposed to be six feet under."

Nick sped up to pass a minivan. In the thickening darkness on either side of the highway, fireflies danced in the summer heat like the blinking eyes of otherworldly voyeurs.

Leon slid a pack of cigarettes from the front pocket of his jeans, didn't ask permission to light up.

Nick glanced over at his twitchy passenger again. "Can I ask you a question, Leon?"

"What's that?"

"Have you ever thought about getting clean?"

Leon blew smoke out through his nose, took three quick puffs on his cigarette before tossing it out the window as if he had never wanted it to begin with. "It's too late for me, hoss."

"Bullshit. It's never too late to try."

"I tried. This one time. It didn't work out so good."

"What happened?"

"Used to have this pit bull. His name was Ron Perlman. Like the guy from *Hellboy*, and that *Sons of Anarchy* show. I love that dude. I loved that fuckin' dog. He was older than dirt, and he was blind in one eye, but he was a good dog." Leon paused, licked his chapped lips. "One night last winter it was snowin' real heavy. I let Ron Perlman inside the trailer so he wouldn't freeze to death. But...I fucked up. I went to take a piss... and that's when he got hold of it."

Nick said, "Jesus Christ, Leon."

Leon's eyes grew wet as he remembered: "I came back in the room, he was lyin' on his side. He was shakin', wheezin', pukin' all over the place."

"He ate your dope."

"The whole bag. I took him to the animal hospital across town. I knew he was dyin' fast, but he was still breathin' so I hoped they could save him. He died in my arms right there in the waiting room. Docs figured out what happened, called the law. They busted me for animal cruelty—like I would ever hurt Ron Perlman on purpose! To make matters worse, they found a bag o' crank in my back pocket that I forgot I had on me."

Nick shook his head.

"Next mornin', Sheriff Mackey comes to see me. He brings this drug counselor geek to my cell. Says he'll drop all the charges if I promise to talk to the guy."

"That was really decent of him," said Nick. "You accepted his offer?"

"I went to see him a few times. But it only lasted through the winter."

"He could have helped you. Why didn't you stick with it?"

"That counselor fella, I didn't like him too much."

"Why not?"

"I didn't care for the way he looked at me. Like he'd never seen anything so sexy. I told him Leon Purdy don't swing that way. But he kept callin' me and callin' me. Said he only wanted to help. Yeah, sure— he wanted to help himself right into my tight lil' butthole!"

Nick said, "It must have been your charm. Your way with words."

"Maybe."

Nick sighed. Wondered how he had gotten himself mixed up with this bizarre little man. And why, stranger still, he actually liked the guy.

"I got one for ya," Leon said. "What's the difference between a crackhead and a tweaker?"

"I give up."

"A crackhead steals all your shit. A tweaker steals your shit then helps you look for it."

That earned a chuckle from Nick. He punched Leon on the arm like two guys who had been buddies forever.

"Ouch," said Leon.

They rode on toward Tryon as the last rays of sunlight died on the horizon. The Bronco's tires hummed on the asphalt. Nick flicked on the vehicle's headlights as he passed a semi with the logo BATESVILLE CASKET COMPANY on its side. He tried not to think about signs and omens. Had never believed in such bullshit anyway.

After a few minutes of silence between them, Leon fidgeted in his seat. He said, "Can I ask *you* a question, hoss? You don't have to answer if you don't want to. Just somethin' I been wonderin'...."

"Go ahead," said Nick.

"You ever think about gettin' revenge for what them fuckers did to you?"

"What?"

"Them psychos that took your face. You ever fantasize about breakin' into wherever they are now, smashin' their heads against the wall till there ain't nothin' left but jelly?"

Nick's grip tightened on the wheel. "I used to. Not anymore."

"I wish I could get five minutes alone with them fuckers. I'd hold 'em down, spit in their eyes! Like you used to do when a match wasn't going your way."

"I didn't really spit in anyone's eye."

"I'm just sayin'. That's what I'd do. For you."

Truth told, while Nick *had* learned to control his rage—accept the things in his life that he could not change, blah, blah, blah—he still wondered on occasion what it would feel like to have his way with the fiends who stole his face. Was a time when he got *hard* thinking about it. These days, though, such thoughts were fleeting when they came. Even if he'd wanted to act on such fantasies, what was he supposed to do—book a flight to Texas, somehow disguise his six-foot-nine, three-hundred-pound frame and stroll through the front gates of the Sharon James Asylum for the Criminally Insane to confront Rebel Yell and One-Arm any time he felt the urge?

He decided to change the subject: "Did you talk to Sophie much?"

"Nah. I dropped by Eddie's place to score, she was always in her room. And when she wasn't, Eddie gave me the hairy eyeball."

"How do you mean?"

"One time her and her mom was headin' out just as I was walkin' up to do some business with Eddie. I asked 'em how they was doin', just makin' polite conversation. Eddie got up in my face, and he said, 'Don't talk to her, asshole. You ain't got no reason to ever talk to her!' I thought at the time he was talkin' about his old lady, but I'd spoke to Melissa before. Later on I realized he meant the kid. I might be a lot of things, but I ain't no short-eyes."

"What about Eddie? Do you think he might have been?"

"Short-eyes? I don't know. But I don't think so." Leon leaned forward in his seat, peered through the windshield. "You wanna take this next exit. We're almost there."

Nick whipped the Bronco over into the right lane, behind a tractor-trailer hauling a trio of yellow forklifts.

"Eddie always seemed super-protective of Sophie," Leon said. "Like he really cared about her. Sometimes I wonder if that's what got him killed that night."

"Funny," said Nick. "I've been thinking the same thing."

"No shit?"

"I don't think those men were there for Eddie. I think they came for Sophie. He got in their way, so they put him down."

"What did they want with her, though?"

"That's the part I haven't figured out yet. But I will."

Neither man said anything else on the matter as Nick steered the Bronco up the exit ramp. At the crest of a steep hill, they came to a Stop sign riddled with BB pellets.

"There she is." Leon pointed straight ahead, to a nondescript building on the other side of a two-lane highway.

"That's it?"

Nick gunned the engine, shot across the road and onto a small lot cramped with perhaps twenty other vehicles. The blacktop was cracked and pitted with potholes deep enough for a grown man to lie down in. The club itself was a small brick building painted forest green with a brown metal roof. The only hints as to what transpired inside were the muffled thump of loud rock n' roll, a neon "Miller High Life" logo in one tinted window, and a sign out front with an arrow that was designed to blink on and off but tonight it just glowed dimly: HOT GIRLS/NO COVER.

To the right of the Skin Den sat a smaller building, this one with boards nailed over its doors and windows. Looked like it might have been a service station at one time. A crooked, hand-painted sign had been erected out front of that place as if in some last-ditch effort to preach to the patrons of the nudie bar next door. It read: UNGODLY MEN GIVE THEMSELFS TO FORNACATION & PURSUE STRANGE FLESH! (JUDE 1:4).

Nick circled the lot once before backing into a space at the rear of the club, next to a shiny black semi.

He turned off the Bronco's ignition, cracked his knuckles. Dabbed at his right eye.

"Let's do this."

His door screeched open.

Leon followed his hero's lead. As they made their way across the lot he devoured his filthy fingernails as if he hadn't eaten in weeks.

✝

As they stepped through the front door of the club, their senses were assaulted by flashing lights, pounding music (currently thumping on the club's P.A. system: "Living Dead Girl"), and the heady smells of beer, cigarettes, and sex.

It was the kind of building that appeared larger on the inside than the outside had suggested. There were two main stages located on opposite sides of the room from one another. On the left, two bored-looking dancers gyrated together to the appreciative cheers of their audience. One of the women had a tattoo on her hip that might have been a majestic phoenix draped in flames, but from a distance it looked like somebody had puked on her and she hadn't gotten around to wiping it off yet. On the stage to the right, a dancer with pale skin and short black hair vied for the attention of the thirty-or-so men in the room, alternately squeezing her tiny breasts together or making them bounce up and down. Only a shaky old man in a rumpled brown suit seemed impressed with her performance at the moment.

Another trio of topless women worked the floor, weaving through the raucous crowd, offering lap dances. Two of them appeared to be identical twins; they sported big 80s-style hair, enormous fake breasts, and orange tans that could only have come from a can.

Nick wasn't sure whom he found more pathetic: the women who

exposed their bodies to strangers for a few lousy bucks, or the men who emptied their wallets for the right to briefly ogle them.

At the back of the room was a long black bar. Behind it stood a thirty-something bald guy wearing a red silk shirt, black leather pants, and a scowl that suggested he was waiting for an excuse to stab someone. Through the thick clouds of cigarette smoke that hovered over the heads of the Skin Den's clientele, Nick spotted a beefy bouncer dressed in black. He appeared to be the only one on duty. He was a stone-faced young man with curly blond hair that didn't fit his tough-guy image. He lingered in a dark alcove between two doorways closed off with velvet curtains, presumably the establishment's "V.I.P." rooms.

One thing Nick found surprising as he made his way through the club was that no one had turned to eyeball *him*. The bartender had given him a sideways glance or two upon first noticing him, as if hoping the big man with the disfigured face didn't crave a drink; otherwise Nick might have been invisible. He doubted it was because of his sunglasses or the hoodie pulled over his head. With so much naked flesh on display, he could have stalked through the Skin Den in his old Widowmaker getup, carrying a gore-streaked battle-axe, and only the bouncer would have paid him any attention.

The heavy metal song segued into a bass-heavy hip-hop tune.

"So what's the plan?" Leon yelled in his ear.

"I'm gonna start at the bar," said Nick. "You talk to the girls."

"Twist my arm, hoss."

"Still got your copy of the photo?"

"Yep." Leon patted his back pocket.

"Take it out, show it around."

"Okay. By the way...you still buyin'?"

Nick pulled out his wallet, thumbed through it. Slapped two ten-dollar bills into Leon's palm.

"Don't spend it all in one place. Remember why we're here."

☩

"Jack and Coke."

"Six bucks."

Nick paid. The bartender got his drink. It was heavy on the flat cola, light on the watered-down whiskey, just as Nick expected.

"So, fella...talk to you for a minute?"

The bartender pretended not to hear him. He had already turned to focus his attention on a muted television behind the bar. Two lightweights were beating the shit out of each other in a bloody UFC match.

Nick pulled out the photo of the man from the drugstore. Slapped it down on the bar.

The bartender didn't even glance at it. He drew himself a glass of water, drank like a dude who had been crawling through the desert for days in search of sustenance.

Louder this time, Nick said, "This won't take long, friend. I just need to know if you've seen—"

"I ain't your friend," the bartender grunted. "And I'm trying to watch the fight."

Nick noticed the way the other man avoided looking him directly in the eyes. When he spoke, he peered at a spot somewhere near the top of Nick's head. Nick resisted the urge to run a hand over his buzz-cut, to wipe away whatever the bartender was looking at. He also resisted the urge to climb up on the bar and piledrive the son-of-a-bitch into that stainless-steel sink.

To Nick's left sat a clear glass jar labeled TIPS. It was empty save for a handful of loose change and a dead spider curled up at the bottom. He wondered if that was why the guy was so pissed off at the world—because his tips jar went largely ignored.

Nick finished off his Jack-and-Coke in two swallows, slammed the glass down on the bar. He removed his sunglasses.

Finally, the bartender turned back toward him.

"Yep," said Nick, "I'm still here."

The bartender glared at him. Or, rather, at that spot on top of Nick's head.

Nick glared back. He tapped the photo between them with one big finger. "Tell me if you know this man. Word is, he's a regular."

"No way you're a cop with a mug like that," said the bartender. "You some kinda private dick?"

"Nope," said Nick.

"What's that make you, then?"

"A guy, looking for another guy."

"What did he do to you, makes you wanna find him so bad?"

"I have reason to believe he took something of mine. I aim to get it back."

The bartender drank more water, looked toward the TV again. The match had ended early; while the ref checked on the unconscious loser, the winner strutted around the ring with his gloves held high.

"I see a lot of people in here. Truckers pulling in, wanna drink a beer and watch some split-tail for a couple of hours. Most of 'em I don't ever see again."

"Like I said, I hear he's a regular. Anybody would recognize him, it'd be the fella pours the drinks. Just look at the picture."

The bartender obviously didn't appreciate being told what to do. Especially by some disfigured freak in an old gray hoodie, looked like he should have been digging through the dumpster out back in search of his next meal.

"If I look at your photo, will you fuck off?"

"Gladly."

He snatched it off the bar.

The change in his expression was subtle. If Nick blinked he would have missed it. But there was no doubt in his mind...

The bartender recognized the guy in the picture.

He let it drop back down on the bar too quickly, sounded *too* sure when he said, "Never seen him. He don't come in here."

"You're sure about that?" asked Nick.

"Yeah, I'm sure." The guy was so full of shit he was swimming in it. "Tough luck. Hope you find your man."

"Thanks," said Nick. "I plan on it."

The bartender feigned interest in the TV again, but when he saw that his fighting show had been replaced by an infomercial he decided now was a good time to start counting the money in the cash register.

Nick put away the picture. Rose from his stool. Leaned against the bar and watched the dancers for a minute as he pondered his next move.

Was a time when he would have honed in like a heat-seeking missile on one of these women. Maybe more than one. They would have left the club together, spent the rest of the night doing things to each other that are still illegal in some states. Now he wished he could tear this fucking place to the ground. Spoil everyone's good time. How dare these people carry on with their petty perversions when a child had gone missing at the hands of one of their own.

One of the orange-skinned strippers approached Nick then, as he was about to step away from the bar.

She pressed her plastic breasts against him, said, "You look like you could use a lap dance, big boy."

Nick peered past her, over her shoulder, mumbled something about how a dry hump was the last thing on his mind.

"Twenty gets ya one song, baby. Don't be shy." Her breath was hot in his ear. It smelled like meatloaf.

"Tell you what." Nick pulled the photo out of his jacket again, held it in front of her face. "I might take you up on your offer, you tell me if you've seen this man."

She stepped back, pursed her lips as she studied the picture. Her eyes were barely visible beneath her heavy black mascara.

"Sorry, sweetie. Can't say as I recognize him. But I just started working here last week. Now, about that dance?"

Nick gently pushed her aside, left her standing alone at the bar.

"...matter with you?" she called out after him. "You ugly *and* queer?"

He ignored her.

He considered trying his luck with the curly-haired bouncer next, but the guy was nowhere to be found. Perhaps he had stepped into the restroom to take a piss, or was busy throwing out some drunk who couldn't keep his hands off the girls. Maybe he was in the restroom *with* one of the girls. And his perm.

Nick cursed under his breath, decided to go look for Leon. He hoped the twenty bucks he had given his companion would prove a worthwhile investment.

Sure. It was probably stuck in some stripper's sweaty thong by now, and Leon's copy of the photo had never even left his back pocket.

✝

If he had turned to shoot the bartender one last dirty look, Nick would have seen the man pull an iPhone from the breast pocket of his fancy silk shirt.

Had he been close enough, he would have heard the bartender tell someone on the other end of the line what had just transpired.

"—thought you'd wanna know. Watch your back."

A pause.

"Yeah, he's still here. I'm looking at the ugly fuck right now. That's right. Blue Bronco with a broken windshield. Parked out back. I seen him walk in with another guy while I was outside having a snort. Hard to miss this freak, know what I'm saying?"

The bartender stuck a finger in his ear, struggled to hear the voice on the other end of the line.

"Well, that's perfect. They could tail him as he leaves the club, lead him right to you. He'll have to take your exit if he's headed back to Midnight."

He poured himself another glass of water.

"Hey, don't mention it. I'm helping out a friend, that's all."

He took a sip. But then he sputtered, almost choked on it.

"Five thousand—? Er...of course I can use the money! Tell Mr. Balfour he's too generous. But he don't have to do that, Charlie. Really, he don't."

A nervous chuckle.

"Of course I wouldn't wanna insult him! Tell Mr. Balfour I'll take his money, if he insists."

†

Nick found Leon in a dark back corner of the club. The skinny meth-head stood with his hands in his pockets, staring up at a blonde dancer who had climbed on top of a table to do her thing. She had big, saggy breasts and a bad overbite, wore nothing but a pair of pink lace panties and silver high-heels. Alice Cooper's "Poison" rocked the club's P.A. system now, but she swayed back and forth slowly, as if moving to the beat of a different tune.

"Yo." A cigarette bounced between Leon's lips. He squinted at Nick through the smoke, said quickly, "We need to talk." A nod toward the girl on the table. "This is Claudette. Ain't she the sweetest thang?"

Nick didn't say anything.

Leon stood on his tiptoes, shouted to Claudette loud enough to be heard above Alice Cooper, "Darlin', this here's Nick, my partner-in-crime."

Claudette leaned over, almost lost her balance. The table wobbled beneath her.

"What happened to your face?"

Nick sensed no cruelty in her question. She seemed genuinely curious. As if she were merely asking him to explain the metric system, or what clouds are made of.

"It's a long story."

"What?" She cupped one hand behind her ear. Nick noticed a tattoo on the underside of her wrist: "JOEY."

When he didn't repeat himself, she shrugged, closed her eyes and went back to her off-rhythm dancing. She mouthed the words along with Alice: *I wanna hurt you just to hearrr you screamin' my name...*

Nick leaned in close to Leon. "Say we gotta talk?"

"Get ready to be happy." Leon took a drag on his cigarette, blew smoke rings in the air. He gestured for Nick to follow him, and they left Claudette behind for now. "You tapped out? Any cash left on ya?"

"Depends on what we need it for."

"Claudette recognizes the man in the picture. Says she'll talk to us, but only in private."

"Great," said Nick. "What time does she get off?"

"Last call's at two a.m."

"I can't wait that long."

Leon shot a glance the bouncer's way. The guy had reclaimed his position between the two doorways with the velvet curtains. "You thinkin' what I'm thinkin', boss-man?"

"I believe I am."

"Problem is, we gotta get by Blondie."

"Why don't you leave that up to me." Nick pulled out his wallet. "How much?"

"Fifty bucks rents the room for half an hour. Claudette's another sixty."

Nick gave him two hundred. "For her trouble. You go in first, I'll catch up."

†

The room was small, dimly lit. To the left of the curtained doorway hung a neon clock urging customers to "ENJOY COORS LIGHT." On the club's P.A. system: the opening chords of "You Shook Me All Night Long."

Claudette straddled Leon on a leather loveseat. Her breasts lay heavy on his bony chest. His forehead was shiny with sweat.

Her long blond hair hung in his face as she whispered in his ear, "So, you and that man with the messed-up face, you were asking about the guy in the picture..."

"Umm, yeah." Leon looked over her shoulder, trying to stall. "Could you hold that thought for a minute, hon?"

The bouncer stood inside the doorway, watching their every move.

"It's your dime, bro," he said, "but the clock's still ticking."

Then Nick entered the room behind him, and the bouncer wasn't saying anything else.

The former wrestler's huge right arm wrapped around the younger man's neck in an old-fashioned sleeper hold. It was a move the Widowmaker had used on a thousand opponents back in the day. Except this time it was real.

The bouncer struggled. Not for long. His knees buckled. Nick maintained the hold for a few more seconds, restricting blood flow to the brain to keep him out for a little while longer. Then he gently eased the bouncer to the floor.

"Diondre!" Claudette squealed.

"He'll be fine," said Nick. "He's just gonna take a little nap while the grown-ups talk."

✝

Leon and Claudette sat beside one another on the loveseat. Nick stood over them. He had removed his hoodie, given it to Claudette. It swallowed the dancer whole. As for Leon, he looked like he'd lost a dear friend when she zipped it up over her breasts.

"Tell us about the man in the photo," said Nick.

She glanced at the bouncer on the floor. "I don't want to know what this is about, do I? You two are gonna get me in so much trouble."

"Please," said Nick. "Help us." He knelt down on one knee in front of her. "It might save a girl's life."

"Anyone I know?"

Nick just stared at her with sad eyes, waiting.

She sighed, swung her legs up into Leon's lap. "I don't know his name. And he don't come in here all the time. But I've seen him. In my profession, you notice guys like him. They stand out."

"How do you mean?"

"He's loaded, that's what I mean. You can tell by looking at him. He wears suits that probably cost more than I bring home in a month. Always smells like he took a bath in the kind of cologne that goes for a hundred bucks a bottle."

Nick felt a chill as he recalled his showdown at the Sunrise Motor Lodge, against a gunman wearing too much cologne.

"He don't throw his money around like a lot of guys, though. He sits at the same table in the corner every time. He orders a couple beers, eye-fucks the girls, but he never stays too long."

"Tell him what you heard that one night," Leon said. "Dude, wait till you get a load of this."

"There was this conversation I overheard between him and another guy," said Claudette.

"When was this?"

"A little over a month ago. I remember 'cause my son's birthday was that weekend. I asked for the night off, but I had to work 'cause one of the other girls was a no-show."

"Who was the other guy? Anyone you know?"

"This guy Eddie who comes in here sometimes."

Leon shot Nick a look, but the big man's disfigured face betrayed nothing. As for Claudette, apparently she didn't know that Eddie had been murdered; she spoke of him in the present tense.

"It was almost closing time. The place had started to clear out. Like I said, the guy in your picture, he usually keeps to himself, but this time Eddie was sitting with him. I walked by their table, and they were arguing. I heard Eddie say something like, 'It ain't right. I made a mistake. I shoulda got that nigger his money some other way.' The other dude stuck his finger in Eddie's face. He said, 'You were the one who came crying to Daddy after that dumb cooze of yours got you in hot water. Now you gotta uphold your end of the bargain!' "

Nick's perfect poker face faltered now. His head hurt as he tried to make sense of everything Claudette had told him.

"Daddy"...there was that weird name again, made even weirder by the fact that it had been spoken by a grown man. Who was he? Some sort of local crime boss? A loan shark with strong paternal tendencies?

What had Eddie promised this man, but then reneged upon? And who was the "dumb cooze" responsible for landing him in "hot water"?

Nick tasted whiskey-laced bile in the back of his throat. He remembered the stuff Sophie had posted online about how Eddie taught her how to fire a gun a few weeks before she went missing.

Was it possible that the piece of shit had *sold* his girlfriend's fourteen-year-old daughter, experienced a change of heart after the fact, but the buyer collected anyway?

"You okay?" Leon asked his hero.

"No," said Nick. "I'm not."

Behind Nick, the bouncer moaned. He babbled something into the carpet that sounded like "jalapeno won't stop nothing."

Nick stepped over him, pinched a nerve in his neck to keep him out for a little longer. He didn't take his eyes off Claudette. "What did Eddie do after that?"

"He just stood up, walked off in a daze. Bumped into me, and it was like he didn't even know I was there. I remember thinking he looked like a guy on his way to the electric chair. Somebody who knows his luck's run out."

"Claudette," said Nick, "have you told anybody besides Leon and me what you heard that night?"

"No," she replied. "It felt like a conversation I ought to keep to myself, you know? None of my business. I've probably said too much already. I've got a little boy at home to think about."

"Joey?" Nick nodded toward the tattoo on her wrist.

She smiled sadly, looked down at the cursive letters under her skin and started rubbing at them. "My baby. He just turned three. He's the only thing that keeps me going, sometimes. Whatever happens, you guys will keep my name out of this, right? You didn't hear nothing from me?"

"You have our word," said Nick.

Leon made a *cross my heart* gesture.

Nick stood, threw a thumb over his shoulder in the direction of the bouncer. "He won't remember much. He'll have a bastard of a headache, but he'll be fine. Tell him you noticed he was looking pale, he complained of a hot flash, a second later he went down. Scared you half to death. You thought about calling 911, but he was only out for a minute."

"Gotcha," said Claudette.

"You're the one who's gonna need 911, girl," said a voice behind Nick then. "What in the blue fuck do you think you're doing?"

"Oh, God...Russo..."

Nick turned to see the bartender stepping over the bouncer.

"What did you tell them?"

Claudette shot to her feet. "I didn't tell them anything! We were just talking."

"You don't get paid to talk. You get paid to shake them big titties of yours. You think our customers would appreciate you blabbing to other customers about them?"

"What's it to you, Russo? You ain't my boss. Why don't you mind your own business?"

"I'm making it my business, whore."

Nick decided he'd had enough of this bastard.

He took two steps across the room, put his fist in Russo's face.

The bartender flew backward as if he had been head-butted by a rhino. He crashed into the clock on the wall, joined the bouncer on the floor.

Nick stood over him. By some miracle, the guy was still conscious.

"Ought to give you some more, for lying to me. You got off easy. I'll be checking in with Claudette. If I hear she's broken a *nail*, I'll be back for you. Understand?"

The bartender made a sound like air escaping from a punctured tire, closed his eyes.

Leon grabbed one of Nick's huge arms with both hands. "We, uh, might wanna go now."

"Probably a good idea."

Claudette unzipped her borrowed hoodie.

"Keep it," said Nick.

They headed for the exit.

†

"Holy shit, that was the coolest thing I've ever seen!" Leon said once they were back in the Bronco. He pantomimed his hero taking a swing at the bartender. "BAM! Motherfucker went *down!* That's what you get when you mess with the Widowmaker!"

Nick started up the vehicle, made for the highway. Narrowly avoided flattening a man who staggered out of the club and into his path. The guy didn't even look up. He adjusted himself through his overalls before climbing into a pick-up with a faded ROMNEY/RYAN 2012 sticker on the back window.

The Bronco's tires screamed like someone being murdered as Nick sped out of the lot.

Leon held on for dear life. He waited till they had merged onto the interstate before asking, "So...Claudette gave us some good stuff, yeah? Something we can use? Did I do good?"

Nick said, "You did real good...partner."

Leon beamed as if he'd just won a lifetime supply of free drugs.

Nick meant every word. He had underestimated the little speed-freak. Expected to walk out of the Skin Den with nothing to show for the trip besides a lighter wallet, a headache from the too-loud music, and maybe a case of blue balls. But his friend had come through for him. He'd had a plan all along. Which was more than even Nick could say.

"What happens next?" asked Leon. "Where do we go from here?"

"I wanna see if this 'Daddy' rings a bell with the sheriff. Maybe he knows somebody who goes by that alias? There's no question he's got Sophie. Only thing left is figuring out who he is. *Where* he is. We're closer than ever, Leon. I'm gonna bring that young lady home to her mama if it kills me..."

"Somethin' else, too," said Leon. "Eddie mentioned a colored fella?"

"He said he wished he'd 'paid him back some other way.' I can't help thinking that ties in with Eddie getting busted earlier this year."

"You lost me."

Nick shook his head. "It's something that keeps picking at the back of my brain. I'm not ready to discuss it yet. And I hope I'm wrong."

Leon frowned, shrugged. Lit a cigarette. The lighter's flame was reflected in his glasses, as if the skinny meth-head's skull had been hollowed out, and his eyes replaced by flickering firelight.

†

The rest of the trip home was mostly silent. Nick didn't mind. It enabled him to mull over everything he had learned.

But as he ascended the exit ramp that would lead them back to Midnight, Leon lit another cigarette and said, "I was thinkin' about somethin' earlier, dude."

"What's that?"

"When all o' this is over, I'll bet you could sell your life story, get them Hollywood suits to make a movie about you."

"You think so?"

"Hell, yeah!" Leon grinned from ear to ear. "Maybe they'd even give me a small part."

Nick glanced over at him. "You wanna be a movie star, do you?"

"Nah. I'm just sayin'. It'd be kinda cool."

"I did make a movie, years ago. You of all people should know that. Once was enough for me, though."

"*Night of the Berserker!* Jason, Freddy, Michael Myers—none o' them pussies had anything on the Berserker! He coulda kicked all their asses with one hand tied behind his back!" Leon exhaled smoke rings as he reminisced: "I remember I was watchin' *Berserker* the first time I got my willy touched. It was at the Lansdale Drive-In. I took Betty Lynn Brubaker to see your movie on openin' night. She had more hair on her arms than me, and she always smelled like sauerkraut, but she was a sweet girl. Anyway...when you busted outta the woods with your meat cleaver and started choppin' up them cheerleaders, Betty-Lynn reached over, put her hand on my crotch, and that was all she wrote."

Nick said, "That, my friend, was too much information. And I'm not quite sure how I feel about it."

"I musta watched my old VHS copy a billion times back in high school. *Berserker* was the fuckin' bomb, I don't care what anybody says."

"It was a bomb, all right," said Nick. "It was a pile of shit."

"I freakin' loved it, man."

"There's no accounting for taste."

At the crest of the hill, Nick rolled to a stop. His fingers drummed upon the steering wheel as he waited for a fleet of rumbling Harley Davidsons to pass so he could turn left.

Leon reached down, turned on the stereo.

"You was born to die," Blind Willie McTell warned the men from the Bronco's ancient speakers. It had always been one of his favorite songs, but Nick killed the music right away. For some reason, the hairs on his arms and the back of his neck suddenly stood to attention.

In his rearview mirror, he saw another vehicle ascending the exit ramp. Coming up fast behind the Bronco.

The approaching car flashed its bluish headlights—from dim to bright, dim to bright—a dozen times or more.

The vehicle veered to the left at the last second, swerving around the Bronco without stopping.

"What the hell?" Nick and Leon said at the same time.

It was a sleek black limousine. A Rolls-Royce Phantom Coupe, to be exact. Nick recognized the make and model because he had ridden in one on multiple occasions. A two-hundred-and-fifty-grand specimen from his ex-employer's private collection had chauffeured him to quite a few GWA promo appearances back in the day. A lifetime ago.

Nick laid down on the Bronco's horn.

The Rolls slid through the night without a sound. Its windows were tinted, but the rear one on Nick's side slowly descended as the limo passed.

Inside, Nick caught a glimpse of an *ancient* passenger: pale, wrinkled flesh...heavy-lidded, piss-yellow eyes...

...and paper-thin lips that peeled back to reveal wet gray dentures, as the senior citizen *smiled* at him.

The limo hooked a hard right in front of the Bronco. A short, sharp squeal of tires, then the fancy car was gone.

The night was silent save for the low stutter-rumble of the Bronco's engine and the chirping of crickets in the tall weeds on either side of the highway.

Nick found himself thinking of that old phrase *the calm before the storm*. He sensed that something bad was about to happen. He didn't know *how* he knew, but he did. As surely as he knew he had two arms, two legs, and a fucked-up face.

"Dude," said Leon. "What was *that* about?"

Nick said nothing. He leaned forward, peering through his cracked windshield into the thick, black night. Steeling himself for whatever came next.

"Did you know that geezer? 'Cause it sure looked like he knew you."

Bright lights suddenly blinded the two men. They came from another vehicle parked across the road. It sat thirty or forty feet away, in a gravel turnaround. Neither of them had noticed it until now.

Too late, Nick realized what was happening. The limo had been trailing them, and its flashing lights were a signal from the first car to the second. A message: *It's them...do it...do it NOW!*

Nick didn't wait around to see what "it" entailed.

He stomped on the Bronco's gas pedal. But the truck was like a hateful woman playing hard to get—she hesitated, shuddered, died.

The other car shot forward. It slewed sideways, blocking the Bronco's path. It was a late-model Mercedes sedan—black, or maybe dark blue.

The passenger-side door opened, and a man stepped out.

"Motherfucker," Nick growled through bared teeth when he saw who it was.

A short, stocky fellow with mutton-chop sideburns, wearing a dark suit with a western-style bolo tie. The man from the motel. The man from the drugstore. The man from the photo in his pocket.

He hefted a doubled-barreled shotgun. He pointed it at the men in the Bronco.

"Leon, get down!"

The shotgun BOOMed.

Nick ducked, felt the windshield crumple in on top of his head like a heavy blanket. Pieces of glass rained down on his neck and shoulders as if someone had thrown a handful of precious jewels into the Bronco's cab.

He fumbled for the keys in the ignition. Turned the switch.

The engine made a sick grinding noise. Caught. Died.

"Come on!" Nick yelled at it.

He heard the man reload.

And then another apocalyptic BOOM ripped apart the night.

Shotgun pellets riddled Nick's left shoulder. At the same time, a thick, hot *wet* splashed across his face. It smelled/felt/tasted as if someone had assaulted him with an old mop. A mop slung from a bucket full of slaughterhouse gore.

Nick's heart pounded in his chest so hard it hurt. A shrill ringing filled his ears.

Beside him, Leon's hands grasped at nothing, fists clenching and unclenching. His long, skinny legs kicked at the floorboard.

Half of his head was gone.

"No! Jesus, *no...LEON!*"

The stench of violent death hung in the air: gunpowder, burned hair, blood, piss, and shit. Pieces of Leon's skull slid down the passenger-side window, dripped from the Bronco's ceiling.

His corpse slumped against the dashboard and lay still.

"Jesus!" Nick shouted again. "Fuck...*FUCK!*"

He blinked his friend's brains out of his eyes. Spat. He could taste Leon in his mouth.

He heard the murderer speak to him then, beneath the ringing in his ears.

"Got word you was lookin' for me! You found me, you dog-ugly piece of shit."

Nick risked a peek through the hole where the Bronco's windshield had been. Saw the man reaching inside his jacket for more shells.

"Your buddy don't look so good. Think he's gonna make it?"

Adrenaline surged through Nick's veins like an illicit drug. He tried the engine again.

The Bronco backfired once, then sputtered to life.

"God damn you!" Nick roared, slamming his foot down on the gas pedal.

The man in the suit looked up from loading his shotgun. He quickly closed the breech, pointed the gun at Nick, but his shot went wild, spraying the Bronco's hood with buckshot.

He screamed as he was pinned between the Bronco and the Mercedes.

Nick stood on the gas pedal. Both vehicles' tires whined against the pavement. The smell of burning rubber filled the air, stronger even than death-stink. The Mercedes rocked on its axels, slid sideways like injured prey falling beneath the weight of a ravenous predator.

The gunman arched his back, twisted from side to side in agony. He pushed against the Bronco's grille as if trying to shove the two-ton vehicle off of him. His fists beat at its hood. His screams echoed through the night.

The Mercedes' passenger-side window exploded. Gunshots *pop-pop-pop*ped as the driver fired at Nick with a small-caliber pistol. The muzzle flashes revealed a man with long blond hair. Lucky for Nick, he was a terrible shot. The Bronco's radiator got the worst of it.

The driver revved the engine twice, threw the Mercedes into gear. Its tires shrieked.

A second later, the Mercedes was gone.

With nothing blocking its path, momentum carried the Bronco forward. Its wheels bounced over the gunman's body.

For a second, Nick's rage nearly got the best of him. He jerked the gearshift into reverse, preparing to run over the man again. But he feared if he started he might never stop—he would keep rolling over the fucker again and again, until he eventually ran out of gas or there was nothing left to roll over.

The Bronco shuddered, then died for good. Smoke billowed up from its hood like the vehicle's soul ascending into the heavens.

Nick sat there for a long time, just staring into his side mirror at the crumpled shape lying in the road behind him. It barely resembled anything that had once been human. But it was still alive. He could see it moving—slowly, and with great effort, but moving nonetheless—in the crimson glow of his brake-lights.

He realized he was hyperventilating. He covered his face with both hands, tried to regain his composure.

He looked to his right, past Leon's still-leaking corpse in its seatbelt. The Mercedes had disappeared into the night as if it had never been there at all. Any effort to catch up with such a machine would be futile, Nick knew. The driver was probably already home by now, feet up, a glass of Dom Perignon in hand.

Nick's head rolled back, and out of him came a deep, tormented bellow. It grew louder, louder, did not stop until his voice grew hoarse and his throat was raw.

"I'm sorry, Leon," he said when that was done. "I'm sorry. They won't get away with this..."

He climbed out of the truck. Winced as his bum knee betrayed him. He caught himself, limped around to the rear of the Bronco.

The hitman's labored breaths sounded like someone sucking mud through a broken straw. He lay on his stomach. Everything below his waist was mangled, smeared across the road. One trembling hand groped for his shotgun a few feet away.

Nick kicked the weapon out of reach.

"Need...ambulance," the hitman wheezed. "Dying..."

"Yep," said Nick.

He had a million questions, but he knew he didn't have much time. "Where is she? Where is Sophie Suttles?"

One eye glared up at Nick. The other stared down at the pavement. The man's thick sideburns were soaked with blood, like strips of maroon carpeting glued to each side of his face. His left ear had been torn off.

Nick pulled his cellphone out of his pocket. "Tell me where to find the girl, I'll have an ambulance here in ten."

The guy coughed blood—along with something solid, long and wormy—onto the ground at Nick's feet.

No way an ambulance would get here fast enough. A hearse would serve him better. Nick suspected the hitman knew it too.

"It's only a matter of time until I get her back. You might as well tell me what I want to know."

The man grimaced at Nick with a mouthful of bloodstained teeth.

"Talk, damn you! Who is 'Daddy'? Was he the old fuck in the limo?"

A moan of pain.

"Eddie Whiteside owed him money, didn't he? Is that why you took Sophie?"

"No...no. Daddy...loaned him the money. To pay the...nigger."

"Tell me who that was!"

The man's eyes closed, and his face went slack. For a few seconds, Nick thought he was gone. But then his eyes fluttered open. He took another rasping breath. Something clicked in his chest, a sound that made Nick think of playing cards in bicycle spokes.

"Give me a name." Nick punched 9-1-1 on his cell, but he didn't complete the call yet.

Another round of thick, wet coughs.

"Eddie call...called him...Coko Puff. Like the...cereal..."

"Once Eddie got his money to pay this person, 'Daddy' wanted Sophie in return? Is that right?"

"That was...the deal."

"Why? What did he want with her?"

"Daddy...likes kids. Always has. And she was...just his...type."

"Jesus Christ." Nick hung his head, thought he might vomit on the guy.

The man took one last ragged breath, and his face fell to the pavement.

†

As Nick watched the chaos around him, he felt like the fattest string on a bass guitar, pulled taut to its limit. Dark blood stained his shirt, and one side of his disfigured face was crusted with gore like warpaint applied by a lunatic. His heart was still racing nearly two hours after everything that had happened.

Sheriff Mackey slipped his notepad back into his breast pocket and asked him, "How many more times are we gonna do this, Mr. Bullman?"

"Do what?"

"Seems people have a habit of dying around you. Violently."

"They started it."

The two men stood on the shoulder at the top of the exit ramp as the lights of emergency vehicles swirled around them. A female deputy directed traffic around the cordoned-off crime scene. In the middle of the barricade sat Nick's battered Bronco. A police photographer leaned through its open driver-side door, snapping pictures. A ponytailed man in an OFFICE OF THE MEDICAL EXAMINER jacket stood nearby, chatting with the photographer as he pulled on a pair of latex gloves. Behind the Bronco lay the hitman's body. It was covered with a thin gray sheet for now. Beneath the bright glow of arc-sodium lights set up along the perimeter, a tall black cop measured the distance between the dead man and his shotgun on the opposite side of the road.

Nick quickly averted his gaze toward the interstate when two officers who barely looked old enough to vote transferred Leon's headless corpse from the Bronco into a body bag. They almost dropped him. One cursed, "Fuck's sake, Freddy, I thought you had his legs," while Freddy looked ready to lose his supper.

"Jesus Christ," Nick hissed beneath his breath.

"I am sorry about your friend," said Sheriff Mackey.

"I can't believe they killed him. He never hurt a soul. He only wanted to help me. He only wanted to make me happy."

The sheriff stared down at his shoes. "He didn't deserve this. Just so you know...I never thought Leon Purdy was a bad person. He was just the type of guy who made a lot of bad decisions."

"I know a little about that myself," said Nick. "Sometimes all a man needs is a reason to change. Somebody to help him be better."

Mackey cleared his throat, changed the subject: "We'll run a trace on the Mossberg first thing in the morning. In the meantime, I've got an A.P.B. out on the Mercedes and the Rolls. Oh, and I almost forgot...I got the autopsy results earlier this evening on our motel shooter."

Nick gave a noncommittal grunt, pulled out his handkerchief and dabbed at his leaking right eye.

"Obviously, we're dealing with twins here," said the sheriff. "But... it's the damnedest thing. The first one, the shooter from the motel? According to the report I received today, he had an old scar that ran from just under his collarbone down to his stomach." Mackey nodded toward the sheet-covered shape in the road. "Our man here, he's got the same scar. I looked. According to the M.E., it appears as if they were *conjoined* twins, once upon a time."

Nick wasn't sure what this information had to do with him. Or why the sheriff thought he would care. Perhaps Mackey expected him to call up Ripley's Believe It or Not, let them know they'd missed out on one more pickled punk for their collection.

"Anyway," said the sheriff, "I have to ask you again. The old man in the limo—"

"*Daddy*. That's what they call him."

"I got that. He didn't say anything to you?"

"No," said Nick. "He just rolled down the window and...smiled."

"He smiled."

"Yeah."

"And you perceived that as a threat."

The big man gestured toward Leon's body bag as it was being carried away, as if to say: *Wouldn't you? Look what happened less than a minute later...*

Earlier, when the sheriff first arrived on the scene, Nick had told him everything. He left nothing out this time. He told him about the name "Daddy" that kept popping up everywhere, and about another player he had recently learned was a part of this twisted game: a black guy called "Coko Puff" who was into Eddie for a lot of money at one time. Something passed across Mackey's face when Nick brought up the black dude, but then it was gone so quickly he wasn't even sure he had seen it. With more than a hint of sarcasm, the sheriff had thanked Nick for sharing the results of his "investigation."

The night had grown strangely quiet now. Things were beginning to wind down, and soon the crime scene would be just another patch of dark country road no different from any other. The broken glass would be swept up. The congealed mixture of spilled fluids—vehicular and human—would be washed away, or would eventually soak into the soil. Inexplicably, Nick found himself thinking of those roadside crosses you see along the highway, monuments marking the sites where loved ones have been lost to auto accidents. Leon wouldn't even get that much. No cheap wooden cross, no wreath of wilted flowers. He would be forgotten. As if the little man had never existed to begin with.

Guilt racked his soul. He clenched his fists, mouthed a soundless curse.

"I promised him," Nick murmured. "He said I was gonna get him killed before this was over, and I promised him that wouldn't happen..."

If the sheriff heard him, he didn't acknowledge it.

A big rig's horn bellowed on the interstate. A man behind the wheel of a massive RV asked the female cop directing traffic at the top of the ramp, "What the hell happened to *him*?" (at first Nick thought he was curious about the corpse in the road, but then he turned to see the traveler pointing *his* way).

Finally, the sheriff told Nick he was free to go. He promised he would be in touch if he had any further questions.

For a minute Nick wondered if he was expected to head back to town on foot. But then Mackey called over one of his deputies, ordered the man to give him a ride back to his motel.

†

Nick couldn't sleep. Not that he wanted to. There would be plenty of time to catch up on his beauty sleep once Sophie was home safe and sound.

Around two a.m. he looked up Midnight Taxi in the phonebook, called for a cab to take him to Eddie's house. He'd been planning a recon mission at some point, still wanted to dig around and see what he could find out there. Attempts on his life kept getting in the way.

He asked the driver to wait. The driver said it wasn't no problem. Nick told him it might be a while. The old guy shrugged, reminded him that the meter was still running, and pulled a dog-eared *Juggs* magazine out of the glove compartment to keep himself company.

Ultimately, Nick's search turned up nothing new. The cops had already taken everything, or there was jack shit to find in the first place. Not a single utility bill had been left behind, no mysterious name or number scribbled on a scrap of paper that might suddenly break the case.

Nick felt beaten, in more ways than one. As he stood in the hallway outside the master bedroom, one hand massaging an ache in his neck while his nostrils itched from the stink of mildewed carpet and rotten goldfish, he thought about Leon Purdy.

He could hear the little weirdo's voice echoing in his head, over and over, as if Leon were right here with him: *I'm a dead man...before all this is over, you're gonna GET ME KILLED...*

Guilt consumed Nick's soul, nearly brought him to his knees. He coughed, and the sound was very loud in the otherwise silent night.

Suddenly his cellphone chirped, vibrated in his hand. He'd been using it as a makeshift flashlight to see his way around the dark house.

When he looked at the display, goosebumps broke out on his forearms: "LEON."

†

"Who is this?"

"Mr. Bullman? Nick Bullman?" It was a male voice. The caller spoke quickly, as if he didn't have much time.

"Who the hell is this? How did you get his pho—"

"Mr. Bullman, listen to me. I have information that I believe will help you find your granddaughter. But you have to do exactly as I say."

"What? Who—"

"Meet me at Washington Park in exactly one hour. Do you know the place?"

"I know it," said Nick.

"You'll find me by the basketball courts. One hour. Come alone, or don't come at all."

The man hung up before Nick could say anything else.

When he tried calling back—again and again, at least a dozen times—Nick's efforts proved futile. Eventually, his calls went straight to voicemail.

†

Washington Park was located in the middle of Midnight's business district. Nick told the cabbie to drop him off in front of Annie's Country Diner. When he was finished here he planned to walk back to his motel, since it was only a couple of miles from the restaurant.

The moon was full and bright. As Nick stalked through the night like a dirty secret, a slight chill in the air made him regret letting Claudette keep his hoodie (Christ, had that only been a few hours ago? So much had happened since his trip to the Skin Den with poor Leon). The streets were eerily quiet. If he had known no better, Nick might have thought he was the only living soul on Earth. A single vehicle had passed him by the time he reached his destination; its high beams flicked on as it sped by, temporarily blinding him. He hoped such a rude deed had at least spotlighted a dose of nightmare fuel for the dickhead behind the wheel.

The park's hours of operation were from sunrise to sunset. The gate was padlocked. After squeezing his bulk between a PARK RULES & REGULATIONS sign and a prickly hedgerow, he accessed the property through a copse of dogwood trees that bordered the main entrance.

He'd been a teenager the last time he stepped foot in Washington Park. It looked nothing like he remembered, was at least three times the size it had been back then. He didn't have a clue where he was supposed to go. Every thirty feet or so a streetlamp lit his way, its bulb softly buzzing overhead. He passed the bandstand, where a banner hung from the gazebo's roof, fluttering in the breeze: FALL CONCERT SERIES COMING SOON – FEATURING YOUR FAVORITE LOCAL GOSPEL ACTS! Then a cluster of covered picnic tables. A small playground. A baseball field that was currently under construction. The air smelled of honeysuckle and freshly-cut grass.

Nick crested a dip in the path, and at last he saw the basketball courts up ahead—four concrete goals around a square of painted blacktop. At first he didn't see the man who had called him here, although he was sure the man saw him. Then a hint of movement caught his eye, and he spotted someone sitting atop a picnic table in the thick shadows beyond the far side of the courts.

For some reason, Nick found himself thinking about his late mother. She had been a fidgety woman, perpetually distrustful of strangers. Although he had come of age in a simpler era—a time when families left their doors unlocked when they stepped out for the evening, a time when children could walk to school without fear of being abducted—he remembered his mother constantly fretting about the motives of any man she didn't know. In her mind, you could spot the villains from a mile away. They dressed in black from head to toe, or wore their hair longer than society deemed acceptable.

Nick assumed it was the sight of his mysterious caller lurking in the darkness that made him think of his mother. Some sort of subconscious trigger. Sitting there within shouting distance of the jungle gym, it was as if the man represented everything Olivia Bullman had taught her son to fear from a young age.

Nick suddenly felt vulnerable. What if this was a setup, yet another attempt on his life? Had he willingly walked into a trap? *Screw it. Too late to turn back now.* If his mother had been right, and outward appearances were the deciding factor, *he* was the boogeyman here. And Nick Bullman could be one scary motherfucker when you backed him into a corner...

The guy stood now, stepped forward, and the light from a nearby streetlamp caught his features. He was a lanky fellow in his late thirties with sandy blond hair and a thick mustache. He wore a checkered flannel shirt, blue jeans, cowboy boots, and a Midnight Mustangs baseball cap pulled down low over his eyes. He had a kind face, albeit a troubled one.

"Mr. Bullman? I'm really glad you came."

They shook hands. The man's palms were sweaty.

Nick said, "And you are?"

"Moseley's the name. Roger Moseley. Sorry about all the sneaking around. But I gotta be careful."

"You look familiar, Moseley," said Nick. "Where have I seen you before?"

"I'm a reserve deputy with the Polk County Sheriff's Department."

"Which explains how Leon's phone came into your possession."

"I was in charge of logging in the evidence back at the station earlier tonight, after everyone else went home. Part of that included documenting the names and numbers saved in Mr. Purdy's phone. Yours was the only one. I took that as a sign. I had to talk to you. Tonight."

"So what is this about?"

The guy removed his cap, ran one hand through his thinning hair.

"Mr. Bullman, I've been struggling with this for a long time. The stuff I'm about to tell you, use it as you see fit. Or don't. Whatever happens, though, I'd appreciate it if you keep to yourself how you came by this information."

"Okay," said Nick. He crossed his arms, waited to hear something useful.

"I overheard some of what you said last night when you gave your statement to the sheriff. You told him that the shooter mentioned a black guy. A fella who calls himself 'Coko Puff.' "

"You know him?"

Moseley reached into the breast pocket of his flannel shirt, pulled out a can of chewing tobacco. "I know him. Every law enforcement agency in western North Carolina knows him. His real name is Clarence Shabazz. He's a known distributor of crack and methamphetamine. A couple months before your granddaughter went missing—this would have been late April, early May—we responded to a domestic disturbance call at the Shabazz residence. When we arrived on the scene, we found a young lady lying in the front yard. She'd been severely beaten. Clarence was inside the house, kicked back, drinking a club soda and watching *The Price Is Right* like nothing had happened. The golf club he had used on his girlfriend was lying across his lap. We arrested him. He didn't resist. He claimed it was self-defense, said his hundred-and-five-pound girlfriend came at him first and he feared for his life."

"This guy sounds like a prince," said Nick.

"You ain't heard nothing yet. In situations like this, we'll typically send in a female officer, she'll try to talk the victim into leaving her abuser. It usually doesn't do any good—we just end up repeating the whole vicious cycle a few months down the road. Anyway...the officer spent some time at the hospital with this young lady, and at some point during their conversation, she said something that got the whole department rattled. She mumbled something about how he 'deserved to burn in Hell for what he did.' She was asked to clarify what that meant, and she said 'he made mad coin off *that girl getting sold*. Doesn't matter *who her granddad is*, she's still just a kid and that shit ain't right.' "

Nick's heart skipped a beat. He would have offered the other man a stunned expression if such a thing were possible.

He settled for a hoarse croak: "What the fuck?"

Moseley flicked his can of tobacco with a middle finger a few times. "We tried to get more out of her, but she clammed up after that. Said she heard him mention it on the phone one night, and that was all she knew. Of course, we proceeded to grill Mr. Shabazz like a summer barbecue."

"And?"

"He said exactly what we expected him to say. He 'didn't know what the hell we were talking about.' Along with some other choice words."

"What did you do then?"

"Nothing we *could* do. This happened months before Sophie Suttles went missing, you understand. We tried cross-referencing the young lady's comment with every missing persons case within a hundred miles, in hope of finding some connection to Shabazz. Nothing came of it."

Nick said, "But when Sophie disappeared, you questioned him again...?"

"We picked him up, interrogated him, held him as long the law would allow. Without any evidence, we were forced to move on. His old lady had recanted her story by then. Sheriff Mackey had that call from Sophie to her mother, from the payphone, so the investigation took a complete one-eighty at that point. The department was no longer looking at your granddaughter as a kidnapping victim, but as a runaway and a possible murder suspect."

The two holes in the center of Nick's ruined face flared like festering wounds.

"The sheriff warned us to stay away from Shabazz after that. Apparently, the feds have been building a case against this piece of crap for the last year-and-half, hoping to send him up once and for all for trafficking. The last thing the boss wants is to shoulder the blame for toppling that house of cards. Shabazz has the best lawyer this side of the state, and he's already threatened to sue the department for harassment. Meanwhile, all we've got is an off-hand comment made months ago by a woman he had just put in the hospital. As much as it pains us to admit it, there's not a shred of evidence that Clarence Shabazz ever laid eyes on Sophie."

"He knows where she is," Nick fumed, more to himself than the other man.

"I'm sure you're right. Unfortunately, our hands are tied."

Moseley put away his can of tobacco then, without ever putting a dip in his mouth. He cleared his throat, peered out into the darkness as if he feared the night had ears.

"However...something you might want to think about, Mr. Bullman: God knows I've lost a lot of sleep with this bouncing around in my head, especially after I heard you'd come to town…"

"I'm listening."

"The law can only do so much. Can't force a man to talk if he don't want to. But there's nothing stopping a civilian from paying this dirtbag a visit. That is, if said civilian knew exactly where to find him."

"I smell what you're stepping in," said Nick. "Tell me where."

Moseley was already reaching into his pocket, pulling out a square of yellow paper.

He placed it in Nick's palm.

†

Nick's mind reeled. Just when he thought this couldn't get more bizarre, some new piece of the puzzle fell into place, forcing him to reexamine everything he had learned up till now.

Doesn't matter who the kid's granddad is…

What the hell was *that* about?

A few minutes shy of six a.m., as the sun began to peek over the Blue Ridge Mountains, Nick stood at a payphone not far from Annie's Country Diner, searching through the Yellow Pages for a place to rent a car. Unfortunately, nothing was open at this hour.

He wondered how long it would be until the Sheriff's Department released his Bronco. Did it even matter, after an assassin's shotgun had turned her front-end into Swiss cheese?

He tried calling Melissa as a last resort, thinking he might be able to borrow her car for a little while. But his daughter didn't pick up.

He cursed, slammed both fists down on the phonebook. The kiosk shuddered beneath his tantrum. A religious pamphlet someone had left there drifted to the ground (DO U WANT 2 GO 2 HEAVEN? asked cursive text above a bad illustration of the pearly gates, and some prankster had penciled a reply at the bottom: "HELLS YEAH!"). A flock of pigeons pecking around a nearby wrought-iron bench scattered to feed elsewhere.

In the distance, a garbage truck *beep-beep-beep*ed as it made its early morning rounds. For about half a second Nick considered hijacking that thing for his purposes.

Realizing he was out of options for now, he stomped back to his motel room. A busy day lay ahead of him. He thought it might not be a bad idea to recharge his batteries with a short nap.

Unfortunately, sleep evaded him like an old friend who owed him money. Nick tossed and turned, stared up at the ceiling as his brain refused to switch to a lower gear. He was dead tired. His body ached from head to toe. But until he had a chance to chat with this cocksucker who called himself Coko Puff, he knew he would remain wide awake.

At precisely eight a.m., he picked up his cellphone and rang the closest car rental company he could find. An hour later, the vehicle was delivered to his motel.

He hit the streets again. This time he took along his tire iron, which had lain beside his bed since the day Melissa invited him over for lasagna.

He only hoped he possessed enough self-control not to hurt Mr. Puff too badly before he got the information he needed.

✝

Nick couldn't recall the last time he had been so uncomfortable. Maybe while he was being tortured by two crazy rednecks who didn't know the difference between real life and sports entertainment. *That* had certainly been worse than this. Or maybe when he'd been kneed in the balls by a soft-spoken hitman with muttonchop sideburns. His current predicament wasn't quite as bad as *that*.

This sucked, though. No doubt about it.

He had asked for *BIG*. Insisted on *plenty of legroom*. Told the rental company he didn't care about *sporty* or even *fuel-efficient*, since he didn't expect to need the car for very long. *Just make sure it's BIG.*

They sent him a Kia Spectra.

A crick burned in his neck. By the time he reached his destination, his spine felt like an old wire coat-hanger that had been bent back and forth until it was ready to snap any second.

Clarence "Coko Puff" Shabazz lived nine miles outside of Midnight, in the southeast corner of the county along the North Carolina/South Carolina border. His house was the last of four on a quiet, dead-end street. It was a small bungalow, gray with blue trim. A satellite dish on the roof. Paved driveway. The property was neatly kept save for a garbage can on the front porch that was overflowing with black bags. To the right of the house, behind a chain-link fence, a vicious-looking Rottweiler sat chewing on a hambone as big as a man's arm.

Nick parked his rental beneath the shade of an elm tree several hundred feet from the drug-dealer's home. He chose a vantage point close enough to spot anyone coming and going, but far enough away so he wouldn't arouse suspicion.

The driveway was empty. Coko Puff wasn't home.

So Nick waited.

†

...and waited some more.

Business must have been booming for Polk County's most prosperous dope-peddler. All day and into the evening Nick watched the house, with only the growling of his stomach to keep him company (how long had it been since he'd eaten? At one point he thought about ordering a pizza, but then decided against it; this wasn't a stakeout in some bad cop movie). Occasionally he tried calling Melissa to give her an update on everything that had happened, but he kept getting her voicemail. More than once fatigue caught up with him, and he nodded off for a few minutes. He cursed himself each time he jerked awake. He sat up in his seat as much as the tiny Spectra would allow, and refocused his bloodshot eyes on the drug dealer's home.

Around three or four in the afternoon, his cellphone rang.

Nick glanced at its screen. Accepted the call. Yawned into the phone: "Sheriff."

"Mr. Bullman. I dropped by the motel, since I was in the area. I was hoping to talk to you in person. You weren't there."

"I stepped out for a bite," Nick lied.

"Mind if I ask what you're having?"

"Annie's." Nick said the first thing that came to mind.

"Hmm. Annie's is closed on Mondays."

Nick was silent.

A radio squawked on the sheriff's end of the line.

For now, Mackey said nothing further about catching Nick in a lie. He wasted no time explaining his reason for calling: "Something I thought you'd want to know. Remember what I told you about the scar shared by our two John Does? I did some digging. Turns out there's an unsolved case from about fifty years ago. Conjoined twins were born to a poor family in Morganville. Boys, attached at the hip. A few weeks after they came home from the hospital with Mom, the infants went missing. There were rumors the parents sold them to a traveling sideshow. The boys were never found.

"Mr. Bullman, I think those missing Siamese twins are the two who came gunning for you. They would be in their fifties now, if they had lived. We've got no priors, no record of your attempted murderers' existence at all. Do you know how rare that is? I've never seen it. Granted, the connection I'm making between an unsolved case from a half-century ago and the guys who tried to kill you...it is circumstantial. But I'll be damned if it doesn't add up. Now I just need to figure out what the hell I can do with this information."

Nick didn't know what to say. He assumed the sheriff expected him to be surprised. But few things surprised Nick Bullman these days.

Mackey apologized then, said he had a call on the other line that he had to take.

"Wherever you are, whatever you're working on, let's pray it leads us to her," he said. "I just want Sophie home safe. All I ask is that you leave a few scraps for me. Something I can put behind bars when this is over."

Abruptly, the sheriff hung up.

For a brief moment, Nick suspected that Mackey knew exactly where he was, what he was up to.

He tossed his phone on the passenger seat and resumed his wait.

✝

Four hours later he spotted his quarry, as the sun began to set.

He heard the car before he saw it. Thumping bass from some hardcore rap song rattled the Kia's mirrors, thrummed through the vehicle's chassis.

A brown Monte Carlo rolled past him. A mid-80s model with oversized chrome rims, windows tinted black as a serial killer's soul. Its vanity plate read KINGPUFF, and a sticker on the bumper urged D.A.R.E. TO KEEP KIDS OFF DRUGS.

Nick couldn't wait to meet this piece of shit. He reached behind his seat to retrieve the tire iron.

The Monte Carlo backed into Shabazz's driveway. The music stopped, but for a minute or more the car just sat there, its engine rumbling like the contented purr of a lion after a long day of slaying weaker animals.

Finally, the driver-side door fell open.

The Rottweiler welcomed its master home with a single bark.

Nick climbed out of the Kia, his stiff old bones popping and cracking like small-caliber gunshots in the twilight.

"Shabazz!" Nick called to the other man. He held the tire iron behind his back, out of sight.

The Rottweiler started barking furiously. It stood on its hind legs, its front claws invoking a metallic song of protest from the bowing chain-link fence.

Shabazz didn't hear Nick at first. He was too busy telling his dog to shut the fuck up. Apparently, the beast's name was Lashonda.

Nick's bum knee throbbed like a son-of-a-bitch as he crossed the road, but he didn't let it slow him down. He only hoped that fence would hold.

"Yo, Clarence!" He refused to call the guy *Coko Puff*.

"Who the fuck are you?"

Shabazz was a short, skinny black man with light skin and long, braided hair pulled into a tight ponytail. He wore baggy blue jeans and a Detroit Pistons basketball jersey. A fat diamond stud glittered in his left ear. He had a bushy uni-brow and a pointy goatee that gave him a slightly devilish appearance. Instantly, Nick knew where the drug-dealer got his stupid nickname: from the cluster of four reddish-brown moles on his left cheek and two more beside his right eye. Most of them were the size of a dime, but a few were as big around as a quarter.

"I need to talk to you," said Nick.

Shabazz looked him up and down.

With one hand he lifted his jersey to show Nick a gold-plated Beretta stuck between his boxers and his washboard abs.

He said, "You might wanna make an appointment next time."

"It's about Sophie Suttles," said Nick.

"What the fuck I care about that bitch?" Shabazz glanced back toward the Rottweiler, licked his lips and gave Nick a taunting grin. "I mean, uh...Coko Puff don't know nobody by that name."

"Wrong answer."

Nick brought the tire iron from behind his back, swung it at the drug-dealer's head.

Coko Puff went down like a spilled bowl of cereal.

He came to slowly, blinking like a man who just stepped out of a dark room into harsh sunlight.

Shabazz moaned. Rubbed at his scalp. The tips of his fingers came away bloody. He tried to sit up, but then hissed through his teeth. He collapsed back into his recliner.

"Shit, man...what hit me?"

Before him, in a straight-backed chair turned backwards, sat the answer to his question. Bigger than life and twice as ugly.

The dealer reached for his gun. Couldn't find it.

Nick showed it to him, before stashing the Beretta between his pants and the small of his back. In his other hand he held his trusty tire iron.

"Who the fuck are you? Somebody send you to rip me off?"

"I think you know who I am," said Nick. "And you can stop pretending that you don't know why I'm here."

The house smelled like Old Spice aftershave and marijuana. The carpet was fancy, snow-white and soft as a kitten's fur, but the walls were painted a gaudy mustard-yellow. Behind Nick, an elaborate stereo system stood silent next to a leather sofa. On the opposite side of the room, atop a small end-table, framed pictures of Shabazz with his arm around a little old lady sat incongruously beneath a poster of Al Pacino wielding an M-16. The way the poster was positioned on the wall, it looked as if Scarface's wrath was aimed right at poor Grandma.

Nick had taken some time to look around the rest of the house while Shabazz was unconscious. He wasn't at all surprised by what he found. A table had been shoved into one corner of the kitchen. The surface was cluttered with miniature scales, glass vials, and plastic baggies. The tools of this scumbag's trade.

"I don't know why you be steppin' up on my property, 'causin' Coko Puff trouble," the dealer said now. "You must be lookin' for some other fool."

"No," said Nick, "I've got the right fool."

"Coko Puff is a peaceful man, yo. I'm a law-abidin' citizen. A follower of Islam. Believe *that*."

"You peddle poison and carry a nine-millimeter," said Nick. "You also have a habit of speaking of yourself in the third-person. Makes me wanna hit you again, hard enough so you don't wake up this time."

Shabazz rubbed at his head again, winced. "You makin' a big mistake, dawg. Don't be surprised if yo' ugly ass wake up dead one mornin', after this."

Nick yawned. "I'm afraid you'll have to get in line, Shabazz. You're not the only one around here who wants to send me home in a box. Besides...look at me. Do you *really* think you scare me?"

Shabazz had no reply.

"Now that we've got that out of the way," said Nick, "I understand you're one of this area's biggest distributors of illegal substances. I have it on good authority that a man named Eddie Whiteside worked for you, before he wound up on the wrong end of a twelve-gauge."

"None of those accusations have ever been substantiated," said Shabazz. "And I don't know no 'Eddie.' "

Nick pointed with his tire iron toward the kitchen.

"The baggies, the vials, the digital scale...I guess those are for selling encyclopedias door-to-door. Cut the bullshit. I'm not the law. I know what you are. But I don't care about that right now. All I want is info concerning the whereabouts of Sophie Suttles."

Shabazz reached into a bowl on an end-table next to his recliner. It was full of those little Valentine's Day candies that come in pastel colors with various flirty messages printed on them. He plucked one out of the bowl, took his time reading whatever it said before popping it into his mouth.

He sucked loudly at the candy, smirking at Nick all the while.

The big man jumped to his feet and hurled his chair across the room. It crashed into the stereo system, shattering the glass door of the entertainment center that housed it.

He brought his tire iron down on the dealer's right arm.

Something cracked. Shabazz screamed—a high-pitched, girlish scream. A rainbow of colored hearts rattled across the end-table like teeth in a bar-fight.

Outside, the Rottweiler started barking like crazy again.

"I'm ready to quit playing games whenever you are!" Nick roared.

Tears filled the dealer's eyes. "I'll talk! Just don't hit me again! Goddamn. I think you broke my wrist..."

Nick shrugged.

"I'll tell you whatever you wanna know. I'll tell you every-fuckin'-thing." Shabazz held his injured arm as he glared at Nick and swore through clenched teeth, "But when all this is over, you better watch yo' back. Believe *that*. I'ma feed pieces of you to my girl outside. You won't be nothin' but dogshit on the muhfuckin' ground by the time I'm done with *you*."

"Okay," said Nick.

"Just tell me what you want and get the fuck outta my house..."

"Last March," said Nick, "Eddie was arrested. He owed you some money after that."

"Eighty large. He had his bitch to thank. She never woulda lost her kid, if her dumb ass didn't do what she did in the first place."

Nick's heart sank. Shabazz was taunting him—he had to know that Melissa was his daughter. But he let it go for now. The dealer had all but confirmed a theory that had been worming its way through Nick's brain the last few days. He didn't want to hear anymore about it from this waste of oxygen. He would ask Melissa for the details, face to face, when he was finished here.

With his good hand Shabazz picked up a piece of candy from the mess beside his chair. His movements were very slow; he was obviously in pain. He read whatever was printed on the little pink heart before slipping it into his mouth. He let out a little moan as he sucked on it, as if the candy helped ease his suffering.

"I gave Eddie one month to get me my dead presidents. After that, Coko Puff had to get nasty. Business is business. Told him I was gonna call up this AIDS-infested nigga I know from the ATL. That mofo, he'll do anything for a rock. I said, 'He'll wait for yo' bitch to come home from work one night, and when he's done with her she won't be good for nothin'. But that ain't all.' I said, 'This nigga, he like a jackrabbit. He don't ever get tired of fuckin'. And he don't care who it is, long as he got a hole to stick his dick in.' I told Eddie, 'Once he's finished with yo' bitch, he's gonna do the same to *you*. Believe *that*.' "

"You piece of filth," said Nick. "I oughta crack open your skull right now."

Shabazz scratched at the cluster of moles on his cheek, winced again as he stared down at his shattered arm. The candy clicked against his teeth.

"So...he paid you back." Nick urged him to continue.

"Coko Puff even made a little profit. For my trouble."

"Where did Eddie get the money?"

"Coko Puff didn't have nothin' to do with that deal, you understand? It was strictly between Eddie and his...benefactor. Once the deal was sealed, though, I guess Eddie started feelin' guilty about the whole thing. Took a likin' to the kid, decided he wanted to play house with her and her momma. He wasn't gonna give her up."

"He died protecting Sophie, didn't he?"

"Looks that way. That dumb mofo even took out an insurance policy on hisself, so they'd be okay after he was gone. I guess he saw the writing on the wall. A few weeks before it all went down, he drove the kid out to the Snake River Woods, spent a whole day teaching her how to shoot."

"How do you know about all of that?" asked Nick.

"Eddie was my friend, yo. We go way back. He confided in me."

"He was lucky to have you." Nick's grip tightened on the tire iron as he loomed over Shabazz. "These people who loaned him the money to pay you back, tell me why they wanted Sophie."

"Not 'people.' One dude. He has his representatives, but it's just one freaky-deak behind it all, from what I heard."

Daddy, Nick knew without asking.

"As for why he wanted her?" said Shabazz. "I hear this cracker got weird...tastes."

Nick's guts roiled as if his insides had been scooped out and replaced with a teeming mass of maggots. "Children. That's what you mean, isn't it?"

"I heard he likes 'em young, yeah. But that ain't the only reason he chose this particular kid."

Nick started pacing back and forth from one side of the room to the other, like an agitated panther, as he listened.

"He collects things," said Shabazz.

"What...things?" asked Nick.

"He's into, like, celebrity shit."

"Movie props? Autographs? What are you talking about?"

"Nah. This ain't the kinda stuff you be findin' on eBay. I don't even know, dawg. Coko Puff just tellin' you what I heard through the muhfuckin' grapevine."

Nick felt closer than ever to understanding everything. "Tell me where I can find him. This...collector."

Shabazz pinched another piece of candy from the end-table. He glanced down at the message on it, but then switched it out for another piece. The saccharine slogan on this one satisfied him, for whatever reason. He popped it in his mouth, sucked on it loudly.

"Now *that*, you gonna have to ask the middle man."

"The middle man?"

"He set it all up. Brokered the deal. Got a finder's fee and everything damn thing, is what I heard."

"Who was that?" asked Nick.

Shabazz bit down on the candy.

"I only met him once. He works at a titty bar not far from here. Dude by the name of Russo."

†

Nick pounded on his daughter's door. "Melissa! Melissa, are you in there?"

A blue-haired old woman in a flowery bathrobe stuck her head out of an apartment down the hall, gave him a pursed-lips expression of distaste.

"Something I can do for you?" he barked at the old bag.

She blanched, shrank back inside.

"Melissa, open up!" He pounded on the door some more.

"I'm coming, I'm coming!"

The sound of a chain sliding back, a deadbolt being unlocked.

She opened the door. She wore a rumpled Waffle House uniform. Her hair was wet as if she had just stepped out of the shower. She was smoking a cigarette.

"What's up, Dad? Is everything al—"

He shoved past her, into her apartment. "Going somewhere?"

"It was supposed to be my night off, but one of the other girls got sick. I offered to cover her shift. Why? What's going on?"

"We need to talk," he said.

She closed the door.

"Any reason you haven't been returning my calls? I keep getting your voicemail."

"I dropped my stupid phone in the toilet." She rolled her eyes. "I was gonna come see you in the morning. Dad...what's wrong?"

"Call me Nick."

"Umm...okay. I thought we were over that. I don't understand, have I done somethi—"

"Leon's dead."

"Oh, my God. What happened?"

"I'll tell you all about it. *After* you tell me what happened last March."

She looked confused. And more than a little afraid of him.

He said, "March thirtieth, I believe it was. The last time Eddie got himself arrested. You know what I'm talking about. The police searched your house, but it was clean as a whistle. They charged Eddie with misdemeanor possession, when he could have been facing felony intent to distribute."

"Oh." She stared down at the glowing orange tip of her cigarette.

He waited.

Finally, she collapsed onto the sofa. A tear trickled down her cheek. "He had two strikes against him already. One more, and they were gonna lock him up for good."

"What did you do, Melissa?"

She took a long drag, blew the smoke out slowly. "I passed the traffic stop on my way home from work. I saw him sitting there on the curb, in handcuffs. He didn't see me. I had my windows down as I drove by. I heard Sheriff Mackey tell his deputies to get to our house right away."

"You panicked," said Nick. "You hurried home and flushed everything you could find."

"Once they came knocking with their warrant, they were too late by *seconds*." She didn't say it as if she were boasting. She merely stated a fact.

"Jesus Christ, Melissa."

She sniffled, wiped her eyes on the sleeve of her Waffle House uniform. "This is all my fault, isn't it?"

Nick gritted his teeth, stared up at the ceiling. Technically, she was right. This all began when she inadvertently caused a drug dealer to lose a lot of money. Never a smart move. But her complicity could not kill Nick's instinct for compassion.

"Come here," he said.

She stood, crossed the room and fell into his arms. "Was it the person Eddie worked for?" she sobbed. "Is that who took my baby? 'Cause I flushed his drugs?"

"No," said Nick. "He got his money. Eddie paid him back with interest before Sophie ever came to live with you."

"Then why—"

"It's complicated."

"How do you know all of this?"

"I had a little talk with Eddie's boss, earlier tonight. Lovely fellow, calls himself Coko Puff."

"So what happens now?"

"Now I have to go."

"Where?"

He pried her arms from around his midsection. "To get Sophie."

†

It was still early, not quite fully dark on a Sunday evening. No more than seven or eight vehicles occupied the club's parking lot.

Perfect. Nick assumed most of the Skin Den's regulars were still in church.

He parked in the front. Left his tire iron in the car this time.

The night was quiet, save for the sounds of traffic on the nearby interstate and the bassline of some hard rock song thumping inside the club. As he stomped across the cracked pavement to the Skin Den's main entrance, the big man was gripped by a surreal sensation that wasn't quite déjà vu. It was something akin to the feeling amputees experience after losing a limb—the "phantom itch" syndrome. He imagined he heard Leon's footsteps behind him, could almost smell a hint of body odor and the smoke from his late sidekick's cigarette on the night's cool breeze.

He swallowed a lump in his throat.

"As God is my witness, I'll make sure you didn't die for nothing," he promised his friend. "I owe you that much."

He didn't realize he had said it out loud until a well-dressed man unlocking his Prius a few feet away turned and asked, "Beg your pardon?"

Nick shot him a look that made all the color drain from the guy's face. He shrank back against his ride.

Nick stood outside the club for a few seconds. Cracked his knuckles. On the door, a sign warned NO CONCEALED WEAPONS ALLOWED ON PREMISES.

He flung open the door and stepped into the Skin Den.

†

Two minutes later, he had Russo the bartender's bald head in his hands, and he was slamming it down on the bar again and again and again.

It felt good. He put everything he had into it, as if there might be some sort of prize at the end.

The dancers screamed. The men in the crowd shouted "what the fuck?" and "think we should do something, Glenn?" But Nick barely heard any of it. A furious buzzing filled his ears, like a swarm of angry hornets, as he bounced Russo's head off the bar. His assault soon fell into sync with the beat of the dubstep tune on the club's P.A. system: *whomp-THUD, whomp-whomp-THUD...*

Finally, someone had the good sense to kill the music.

The bartender called Nick a motherfucker as his head came up again. That's what it sounded like, anyway. He might have asked the big man to name his favorite action flicks. His lips were busted open like smashed grapes, two of his front teeth lay next to his empty tips jar, and his voice was all but unintelligible.

"You and me, we need to talk," said Nick. "You're gonna tell me where I can find Sophie."

"I don't have to tell you a goddamn th—" Russo started to say, but then Nick jerked him over the bar as if he weighed no more than a jug of that watered-down horse-piss he served his customers night after night.

"Better yet, you're gonna take me to her. Let's go for a ride, asshole."

As Nick headed for the exit, he saw the curly-haired bouncer running toward them.

He glared at the guy. Slowly shook his head, like a stern parent warning a child not to act up in public.

The bouncer changed his mind, melted back into his dark corner.

"Who the hell do you think you are?" a voice screeched in Nick's ear. "You can't come in here throwing your weight around like that!"

Nick turned to see one of the orange-skinned, fake-tittied strippers from the night before. The one who had accused him of being gay because he didn't want a dry-hump.

"You're just a big, ugly bully," she said. "That's all you are!"

"Maybe."

"You look like my cousin's retarded stepson."

"That hurts," said Nick. It didn't.

"I'm calling the cops."

"Why don't you go ahead and do that, honey? Tell them your buddy here was involved in the abduction of Sophie Lynn Suttles. Tell them he's seen the error of his ways, and he's gone to get her back."

"Don't," the bartender said. "Leave it, Sheila. Don't call the cops. It's gonna be okay."

The expression on the stripper's face was that of someone who is unsure if she has chosen the right path in life. She backed away from Nick. Another young woman sobbed at the rear of the crowd.

"You're making a big mistake," the bartender told Nick. He wore a piece of tape on his nose from their last altercation, but it had come loose. It dangled from his cheek like a flap of dead skin. A bright red bib of blood stained his once-white TAPOUT T-shirt.

Someone else rushed at Nick then.

This time she wore a thin white blouse unbuttoned to her belly and a checkered "schoolgirl" miniskirt. Her blond hair was tied back in a ponytail.

"Claudette."

"I wanted to tell you...he hasn't laid a hand on me. Hasn't spoken to me at all, after what you said to him. It's like he's scared of me."

"That's good to hear," said Nick.

"I thought you should know. I'm fine." She touched Nick's arm. "Are you...gonna hurt him?"

"Probably," said Nick. "He's done some bad things. You'll hear about them soon."

Claudette looked at the bartender. He hung his head.

Nick gave a barely perceptible nod to the young lady, before shoving Russo toward the exit.

✝

"What do you drive?" he asked, once they were outside.

"The red Camaro."

Nick glanced toward his Kia parked a few feet away. "We'll take yours."

✝

Russo drove. Nick sat beside him in the Camaro's passenger seat.

For now, he had instructed the bartender to drive toward Midnight. As they merged onto the interstate, he said, "Tell me what you did."

"Go to hell."

"Start over."

Russo winced, made a pained grunting sound.

"You sold her like she was a piece of property," said Nick.

"I introduced one guy to another guy. That's all. Maybe I made a few bucks off the deal. Whatever happened after that, I didn't have nothing to do with it."

"How did it go down?"

Russo watched the rearview mirror as if expecting to find the answer there. While he waited, blood dripped from his broken face onto his leather-clad lap: *plip-plip-plip*, like ellipses in their conversation.

"I'm not gonna ask you again," said Nick.

"There was this guy Eddie, used to hang out in the club sometimes. One night he's knocking back shots of tequila like it's nobody's business. I ask him what he's trying to forget. He starts rambling on and on about he owes this nigger a lot of money."

Russo brought a hand to his shattered nose. Rolled down his window and spat bloody saliva out into the cool night air. Most of it blew back in his face. He rolled up the window.

"Keep talking," said Nick.

"He says if only his girlfriend was still in touch with her daddy. Maybe he could squeeze some dough out of that fucker. Guy used to be a famous wrestler."

Nick's disfigured face betrayed nothing.

"I call over this fella I know. The, uh, one in your picture. He works for a private collector. Celebrity stuff. The more fucked-up, the better. The Widowmaker's story, that's about as fucked-up as it gets, right? I don't have to tell you. Yeah...according to this Eddie guy, she's your granddaughter. And she's barely old enough to bleed. I figure she'll be worth a ton of green to a rich prick with a touch of the 'short eye.' Turns out I'm right. He can't wait to add her to his collection."

It took every bit of willpower Nick possessed not to throw Russo out of the car at that moment, like a litterbug chucking a hamburger wrapper. He restrained himself, but just barely.

Russo tightened his grip on the steering wheel, as if he could read Nick's mind.

Nick said, "You're talking about Sophie like she's a tube of lipstick used by Marilyn Monroe, or an old napkin Sammy Davis, Jr. sneezed on. You can't 'collect' a human being, keep her in a glass case in some fucking museum."

"You can do whatever you want when you've got more money than God," Russo replied. "This guy does."

"What's his name?"

"Mr. Balfour. Hiram Balfour. But his associates all call him—"

"Daddy," said Nick. "I know. Where does this asshole live? How far do we have to go?"

"I don't know where he lives. Somewhere in Morganville, I think. But I've never been to his house."

"Did you think we were just gonna drive around, maybe I'd get sleepy and nod off after a while?"

"You told me to drive. That's what I'm doing. I can't tell you where to find him because I don't know."

"You also claimed you didn't know the guy who robbed the drugstore."

"He was my only link to Mr. Balfour. But he can't help us. Because you killed him."

"Correction," said Nick. "I killed *both* of them."

The bartender cursed Nick beneath his breath.

"Sounds like you expect me to apologize. I must have misunderstood his intentions after he repainted the inside of my truck with my buddy's brains, then tried to do the same to me. As for his brother, I guess he broke into my motel room looking for some *other* seven-foot, three-hundred pound guest with a face like a slab of roast beef left out in the sun."

Russo was silent.

"What was his name?" said Nick. "Your friend."

"Charlie."

Nick brought a hand to his face, pinched at the gnarled scar tissue that had once been the bridge of a strong, Roman nose as he took a minute to ponder his next move. It was a no-brainer that Russo was the one who had tipped off the assassin last night. He assumed that had happened well before he and Leon left the club. However, he recalled Sheriff Mackey telling him that the off-ramp hitman had nothing on his person but the twelve-gauge, which meant that Charlie's cellphone—assuming he had owned one—was most likely in the hands of the wheelman now. The driver of the Mercedes.

It was worth a shot. Perhaps it would amount to nothing, but Nick had a hunch...

"Your phone," he said. "Give it to me."

"What?"

Nick didn't repeat himself. He held out an open palm.

Russo's hands shook as he pulled an iPhone from a pocket in his leather pants. He gave it to Nick, begrudgingly.

Nick thumbed through the bartender's contacts. Lots of women. Most of them with stripper names: CANDI, MITZI, DEEDEE, MONIQUE. Although a MEEMAW was in there too.

Finally, Nick found what he was looking for: CHARLIE.

He handed the phone back to Russo. "Call it."

"What? But...he's dead. You ki—"

Nick glared at him.

Russo did as he was told. He put the phone on SPEAKER so Nick could hear both sides of the conversation.

The call went straight to voicemail. A beep, then a man's voice said, "Leave a message. I'll get back to you if I think it's worth my time."

"Umm...yeah," the bartender said into the phone. "It's Russo. Charlie's friend from the club. If, uh, anyone's still checking his messages...we need to talk. It's about the kid. It's...not good."

He hung up, set the phone on his knee.

"What do we now?" he asked Nick.

"We keep driving. And we wait for someone to call us back."

†

Ten minutes later, the phone rang. The ringtone was something by Lady Gaga.

Russo shot Nick an embarrassed look.

The big man didn't blink. "It's not gonna answer itself."

Once again, it was a man's voice on the other end of the line. But a different one this time.

He said, "You shouldn't be calling this number. You don't have any reason to be calling here anymore."

"Wait...wait!" Russo shot a nervous glance toward Nick. "There's,... uh...something you need to know."

"What is it?"

"Tell him the Widowmaker is coming," said Nick. He stared straight ahead as he spoke. "His people tried to put me down for the count, but they just pissed me off. If we have to drive around all night, we will find them. Morganville's a small town, and they should know by now that I don't give up easily."

"Umm...I guess you heard all of that?" Russo said into the phone.

Silence. A silence that seemed to last forever. No, not quite silence. Faintly, there was muffled conversation on the other end of the line. It sounded like the man had covered the phone with one hand and was arguing with someone in the background.

Pavement hummed beneath the Camaro's tires. At least a minute passed.

Russo swallowed loudly, asked, "Are you still there?"

"There's a place in Midnight. Storch's Rim. Do you know it?"

"No," said Russo.

Nick said he did.

"Be there in half an hour. Just the two of you. I see anybody who looks like a cop anywhere near the 'Rim, I will slice off one of her tits."

The connection was severed.

Nick spat out every obscene word he knew. His massive fist struck the dashboard again and again. When his assault was finished, his knuckles were bloody and raw. The dashboard fared no better. The door to the glove compartment fell off, landed between his boots as if it were made of cardboard.

Russo, meanwhile, now looked as if he might be thinking about throwing *himself* out of the car, just to get away from the giant's fury.

⸸

Once upon a time, Storch's Rim had been Polk County's own Lover's Lane, its "make-out spot" where Midnight's teen contingent sneaked away to park late at night and indulge in forbidden activities. Nick Bullman remembered it well. He had lost his own virginity there forty-some years ago, to a young lady whose name he had long since forgotten. Back then, the 'Rim had been an eyesore of the worst kind. Strewn throughout the grove atop the region's highest point of elevation was the detritus left behind by those who cared about nothing more than having a good time: crumpled beer cans, shattered liquor bottles, and the occasional used condom. A lot had changed since Nick last saw the place, however, and for the better. Instead of hard-packed earth cross-hatched with dozens of tire tracks, a circle of white gravel welcomed visitors to the lookout spot at the end of a winding blacktop road. Picnic tables had replaced the graffiti-stained boulders that once bordered the parking area. A yellow guardrail had been erected at the edge of the 'Rim, protecting those who came here from certain death. Beyond it was a steep drop-off that might have been the very edge of the world. Those who stood at the top of the 'Rim could see for miles and miles. Below, the distant lights of Nick's hometown resembled a multitude of bright, unblinking eyes in the night.

Nick ordered Russo to park along the edge, but told him to back into the spot, so they could see the enemy coming. The only sounds were the urgent chirping of crickets in the thick brown weeds upon the mountainside and the whisper of a soft breeze wafting through the nearby treetops. A hint of lightning flickered in the clouds above town every few seconds.

At one point, Russo asked Nick if he could leave. He promised he would just get out of the car and start walking, he wouldn't even look back. This didn't have anything to do with him anymore, he said, and he just wanted to go home.

Nick told him to shut his fucking mouth, don't move a muscle, or it would be his name on the MISSING posters all over town come tomorrow.

They sat in silence the rest of the time.

No more than fifteen minutes later, headlights appeared on the road.

The vehicle crested the hill, blinding both men with its high beams.

"You get out," said Nick.

Russo gave him a look like he had just been instructed to climb over that guardrail and take flight over Midnight.

"Get out," Nick said again.

Gravel crunched beneath the other vehicle's tires as it came to a smooth stop about a dozen feet in front of them. It was something large. An SUV, for sure. A Hummer, maybe.

Russo stepped out of the Camaro.

A tall, man-shaped figure got out of the SUV, on the driver's side. He left the engine running.

Russo glanced over at Nick, as if waiting to be told what to say. "H-Hey...he made m—"

One of the silhouette's hands came up, and three quick pops shattered the quiet night. Muzzle flashes.

Blood spurted from Russo's throat and chest. He made a choking sound, and was dead before he hit the ground.

Nick threw open his door.

"Stay where you are!"

The shooter approached him, stuck a small pistol in his face. Nick still couldn't make out the man's features, as the man stood between him and the SUV's high beams. He could make out long hair, what looked like an oversized leather jacket, but not much else.

"Hold out your right hand."

Nick did as he was told, tentatively.

The man slapped a cellphone into his palm. "It's for you. Don't keep him waiting."

Nick brought the phone to his ear.

"Nicholas James Bullman," said a voice, with what sounded like great effort. "A.K.A. 'the Widowmaker.' Sports entertainment's brightest star...until they took your face."

The voice was ancient, decrepit. Nick didn't hear it as much as it seemed to *slither inside* his ear, like something diseased and eager to infest.

"And you must be Mr. Balfour," said Nick. "The one they call 'Daddy.' "

"Ah, so you know who I am," said the old man. He spoke very slowly, in an almost robotic manner, carefully enunciating every syllable. "My associates and I should have known better than to underestimate you. You have caused us an unprecedented amount of trouble." A long, rattling breath. "Mr. Bullman, I wish for you to come see me. Tonight."

"I look forward to it," said Nick.

"You will ride with my associate. If, at any point, you act in a manner unbecoming of a guest on my property, he will not hesitate to put a bullet in your brain. Do you understand?"

"I understand," said Nick.

"Wonderful. Goodbye for now, Mr. Bullman. Please give the phone back to Jeremy."

"I'm assuming you're Jeremy." Nick handed the phone to the man standing over him.

The gunman brought the phone to his ear. "Yes?" He listened. "Okay."

He hung up.

"Out of the car."

Nick stepped out of the Camaro with his hands in the air.

"Now get in the Hummer." The man gestured with his weapon for Nick to walk in front of him.

Nick did as he was told.

The man followed him, slammed the Hummer's passenger-side door once Nick was inside.

And suddenly Nick felt a sting in the back of his neck. As if from a giant bee perched on his shoulder. Took him a second or two to realize it was a needle. Something burned through his veins.

He tried to turn, to rip the spike from his flesh and fight off the culprit, but already his head felt as if it had swollen to the size of a hot air balloon. His arms weighed a thousand pounds each.

"Don't try to fight it, handsome," said a voice behind him. "Won't do you any good. We just need you docile for the next few hours. Like a big ole' puppy-dog..."

A laugh from the man with the gun, as he slid behind the wheel. For the first time, Nick caught a glimpse of his face: tan skin, very white teeth, long blond hair. He watched Nick lose consciousness as he pulled on a pair of fancy leather driving gloves.

How could you let this happen? Nick asked himself, but the thought was strangely disassociated, as if it didn't come from his own brain at all. As if he were just now recalling an old friend with a speech impediment asking him the question six years ago.

Someone in the backseed...now you been drugged...and you think you're gonna saaave her? Stooopid...mother...fugggggggg...

The world dropped out from under him then, and everything went black.

†

The hum of tires on pavement. A dry cough. Someone complaining about the President on a talk radio station turned low.

Nick floated in and out of consciousness. He dreamed he lay in a tiny boat under a starless night sky; the tide kept pushing him to shore then jerking him back out to sea before he had a chance to step foot on solid ground. He sensed he was sprawled in the Hummer's backseat now. How much time had passed? Impossible to tell. He felt heated leather seats beneath him, smelled pine-scented air freshener. Two large human shapes sat up front, silhouetted against the green glow of the dashboard lights. He could hear snippets of conversation, but their voices were oddly muffled, as if a thick wall of cotton separated the big man from his abductors.

"He's waking up. Reckon you oughta dose him again?"

"Better not. Even at his size, too much might kill him."

"What was that stuff again?"

"Ketamine. It's a horse tranquilizer."

"Where in the world did you get something like that?"

"I used to date a veterinarian, remember? She was from Taiwan. It's big in the rave clubs over there. After hours, the doc was a real party girl. I sure do miss her. The things she could do with that mouth..."

"Oh, hell—would you look at that! He fucking puked! He's making a mess of my seats."

"Look what he did to my Mercedes, no thanks to you."

†

"What the hell is he saying back there?"

"Sounds like he's *singing*."

Nick heard it too, as he briefly came awake again. The singer was tone-deaf, couldn't carry a tune in a dump-truck.

Then he realized it was his *own* hoarse voice butchering his favorite John Lee Hooker song.

"Serves me right to suffer," he babbled along with the blues on the stereo.

But the SUV's radio was still tuned to a talk station. The music was a figment of his delirium. Nick knew this. Yet somehow, at the same time, he couldn't fully comprehend it.

He made a farting sound with his mouth, fell back into the pitch-black waters of unconsciousness.

†

A turn signal *tick-tick-tick*ed. Gravel crunched beneath tires. Crickets chirped through an open window.

"Ever wonder if it's worth all this?"

"What do you mean?"

"I mean...the Charlies are dead. And for what? We both know the old man's mind ain't what it used to be."

"Watch your mouth, Jeremy. It's worth it to Daddy. Nothing else matters."

The duo rode in silence for a while. For five minutes, maybe. Five hours. Perhaps for several days. Nick couldn't tell, as he continued to drift in and out of consciousness.

Then: "It could be a long night, you know. There's one more thing we'll need to do before we can close the door on this mess once and for all."

"What's that?"

"When we get him back to the house, we're gonna have to...do stuff to him."

"Something tells me you're not talking about giving the guy a makeover."

"No. Although he could use it. We're gonna rip out his fingernails, blowtorch his balls, whatever it takes to find out where his daughter is staying."

"Sounds like a party. So...we're torturing people now?"

"Getting an attack of conscience all of a sudden, Mr. I'll-Slice-Off-One-Of-Her-Tits?"

"I was only trying to scare him. Playing a role."

"I'm not crazy about the idea either, Jeremy. But it's a necessary evil. The twins should have cleaned up all the loose ends to begin with. They didn't. Now they're dead. So we're forced to get our hands dirty."

"That's why you told me to pop the guy in the Camaro. He was a loose end. I get it now."

"Like I've said before, Daddy should have put me in charge of this whole thing from the start."

"I'm with you there. When you wrote that script, forced the kid to call her mom and read it? Frigging brilliant."

"It worked until this asshole came to town and started stirring shit up again. Daddy sent Charlie One to take care of business, but he never had the stomach for stuff like this. Then Two panics 'cause of one little seizure. Pulls his stunt at the drugstore, gets his mug plastered all over the news. Unbelievable."

The screams of multiple sirens passing in the night. A chorus of emergency vehicles, fighting to be heard over one another. Rising then fading in the distance, Doppler-style...

"There they go."

"Look at what you started. When you threw him in the Camaro, torched it and drove it off the edge of the 'Rim? Watching you work...it was like fucking *art*."

"I don't know about that. I just did what had to be done."

"Have I ever told you that's what I love most about you?"

"Feel free to tell me again."

"You can be one ruthless cunt when you wanna be, Little Sister."

†

His brain was a cantaloupe gone soft with rot. Even after he was fully awake and—for the most part—had his bearings, he couldn't quite make out the features of the two people standing over him. His vision blurred, focused...blurred, focused...as if he were watching an amateur film shot by a cinematographer who didn't know what the hell he was doing.

"Ya know," said a voice, "now that I get a good look at him...whoa. I never expected it to be this bad. He is the *definition* of *ugly*."

"You can say that again," said another voice.

"I mean, how do you go through life looking like that? I'd never leave the house. Probably woulda slit my wrists the first time I looked in a mirror."

"Yeah, but you've always been a little vain, Jeremy. You spend more time fixing your hair than most lipstick lesbians I've known."

Whatever Nick was sitting in—he got the vague impression of a large wooden chair with soft, cushioned seats—rocked from side to side as one of the figures kicked it.

"Bullman. Hey, Bullman. You awake?"

"Rise and shine, handsome."

"I'm awake," said Nick.

"I was just telling my sis here...I didn't realize till I saw you up close how hideous you really are," said the one named Jeremy. "Know what you remind me of? A shaved ape. No, wait...a shaved ape with Down's Syndrome."

"After a really bad car accident," said the one called Little Sister.

They laughed together. Loudly. Cruelly.

Nick found himself chuckling with them. He was still feeling the dissociative effects of the drug the woman had dosed him with. As if this were happening to some *other* guy while he watched. He felt sorry for the poor bastard. Was rooting for him all the way.

He said, "I didn't just fall out of the ugly tree and hit every branch on the way down, right? I planted the tree, watched it grow, then one day the fucker fell on top of me."

If you can't beat 'em, join 'em...

This all felt like some surreal fever dream. A remix of the song of madness Rebel Yell and One-Arm had composed for him three years ago. Nick was gripped by a feeling of déjà vu stronger than any he had felt before. He almost expected those two cackling, black-and-white-striped fools to enter the room any moment, and finish what they'd started that night in Amarillo.

He shuddered. His teeth chattered, although he wasn't cold.

At last, his vision fully cleared, and he was able to get a good look at his abductors...

The man was thirty-something, tall, broad-shouldered. He wore a purple dress shirt with the sleeves rolled up, and lots of gold: several rings, a hoop in one ear, a wristwatch that probably cost more than Nick's late Bronco. His straight blond hair fell halfway down his back. His long hair and bronze skin gave him the appearance of a surfer dude dressed up for a court appearance.

The woman wore a charcoal suit over a blue dress shirt and a thin, silvery tie. The suit was a size too small. Her body rippled with more muscles than Nick had ever seen on a female. Veins stood out on her neck and wrists like worms trapped under her skin. She wore her hair in tight cornrows. On her left cheek were three long, scabbed-over scratches.

Somehow, Nick's drug-addled brain put the pieces together: he remembered Leon telling him how he had witnessed Sophie "clawing one of the big dudes in the face" the night she was abducted. Here was the "big dude" in question, he assumed. An honest mistake.

That's my girl, Sophie...I hope it hurt like hell...

Nick took in his surroundings. He sat in a small, square room with cream-colored walls and plush carpeting the color of blood. An expensive-looking lamp sat on an end-table in one corner, beneath a framed print on the wall: a black-and-white photograph of the Hollywood sign circa 1970 or so, when the famous landmark was in dire need of repair. Otherwise the room was empty. Just Nick and his new friends.

"How are you feeling?" Jeremy asked him.

"Like a pile of dogshit that's been stepped in and smeared around," said Nick.

"Funny. You look like it too."

Nick scowled at the younger man, but then he laughed too. He wished he could stop doing that. He felt like a teenager after his first sip of beer or toke of wacky weed. Whatever the bitch had dosed him with, he had to admit it was some really good shit.

And then he wasn't laughing anymore...

Little Sister's fist was like a boulder in his face. She stepped forward, hit him with a massive right hook that would have impressed Nick under different circumstances. He never saw it coming, and didn't think he had ever taken such a punch. Maybe that one time, when...no, that just happened. He was already flashing back to *this*, here, now. Damn, the stuff in that needle had really fucked him up. He could barely differentiate between up and down, left and right, or the present versus fifteen minutes ago. Kaleidoscope colors flashed before his eyes, and for the next few seconds he couldn't feel the bottom half of his face.

"What'd I do to deserve that?" Nick asked through a mouthful of blood.

"That was for Charlie One," she replied, "and *this* is for Charlie Two..."

She leapt into the air, caught him in the nose with a brutal roundhouse kick.

He was surprised she didn't knock his head completely off his shoulders that time. A few more of those, Nick was quite sure his skull would go flying across the room like a battered old basketball with eyes, and it would *splat* against that picture of the Hollywood sign on the wall.

He blinked. Cursed. Spat a glob of blood onto their fancy carpet.

"How do you like that?" Jeremy asked him.

"Didn't care for it much," said Nick.

"You're gonna like it a lot less before the night is over," said Little Sister. She asked her brother, "What about you? Do you want to get a few in?"

"I'm good for now."

"This guy killed the Charlies. He cut our family in half, like *that*." She snapped her fingers, and the sound was very loud in the small room.

"Maybe later."

"Suit yourself."

"Enough," said a new voice behind the siblings. An ancient, rasping voice like dead leaves rustling in a dank crypt. "I know you kids are enjoying yourselves. But Mr. Bullman is our guest. He deserves to be treated as such...for now."

The two quickly stepped aside, so the big man could see who sat there in the doorway. Although Nick already knew.

"Bring him downstairs, please. It isn't often I get to show off my collection. I am very much looking forward it. And there is someone who is dying to meet him."

"Yes, Daddy," said the siblings.

†

"Where is she?"

"In due time, Mr. Bullman. In due time."

"I want to see her. I want to know she's okay."

"I didn't live to be ninety-three years old by being impatient. You could learn a few things from a man like me. I assure you, the child is safe."

"Take me to her," said Nick.

"Soon."

Hiram Balfour rode along in a motorized wheelchair that hummed softly across hardwood floor. A wrinkled green pajama suit swallowed his gaunt frame. A few thin wisps of snow-white hair sat atop his wrinkled head. The old man's flesh was covered with liverspots. One spidery hand lay in his lap like a dead bird; the other gripped the controls of his chair like a demon's claw wrapped around the throat of a small child.

They headed down a long hallway. Little Sister walked beside the old man, a bizarre sight in her cornrows, too-small suit, and bulging muscles. Jeremy walked behind Nick. While Nick was still a bit unsteady on his feet, the drug had gradually begun to release its hold on him. Little Sister had suggested they cuff him, but the old man said that wouldn't be necessary.

They passed a tall archway on their right, through which Nick caught a glimpse of the house's main foyer. He got the impression of extravagance, unimaginable wealth, a residence larger than any he had ever seen. Marble floors. Ornately-carved banisters. Cathedral ceilings and immense crystal chandeliers. From somewhere in that part of the house, "Fur Elise" played on what sounded like a scratchy old Victrola.

"Forgive me if I do not show you the rest of the house," said Mr. Balfour. "I know you do not care about any of that anyway. You are here for one reason, and one reason only."

"You've got my number," said Nick. His heart raced as he knew he was coming closer and closer to seeing Sophie for the first time.

When they reached the end of the hallway, they entered an elevator. It was small, cramped. All four of them fit inside, but just barely. Nick stood beside the old man's chair, looking down at the top of his skull.

It would be so easy to end this...right now...

No. Gotta find Sophie first. Let them lead me to her. Get the child out of harm's way. Then...and only then...

Little Sister pushed a button. The elevator door closed.

They went down.

The old man stared straight ahead as the elevator descended. His breaths were very loud in the confined space. He wheezed like something choking out its final death rattle.

Nick said, "I'm guessing this is the part where you spend the next twenty minutes boring me with your nefarious plan."

"I beg your pardon?"

"Isn't that usually the villain's downfall?"

Mr. Balfour laughed. It was an obscene sound, like a mold-covered door creaking open to reveal a cellar full of rotting corpses. "That would assume I am the villain here. Which is a matter of perspective. I have no 'nefarious plan.' I am simply a man who is proud of his collection, and wishes to show it off to a guest in his home."

The elevator stopped.

"And here we are..."

The elevator door opened. Little Sister stepped out, flicked a switch on the wall.

Fluorescent lights flickered on.

Before them was a rectangular room, its walls and floors painted a uniform gray color. Two long, gray metal shelves traversed the length of the room, both of them nearly as tall as the ceiling.

Mr. Balfour said, "You've heard of Robert L. Ripley, I'm sure? Of *Ripley's Believe It or Not?* He has long been a personal hero of mine. In fact, it was reading about Ripley and his adventures throughout the world when I was a much younger man that started my...obsession...in the first place."

"What is this?" said Nick.

"There was a time in my life when I collected...oddities of nature, if you will. Freakshow abnormalities. 'Pickled punks.' The practice of preserving and displaying these poor souls has been around for centuries, starting with King Frederick III of Denmark, whose collection numbered in the thousands. Throughout the years, I discovered that many of them were gaffes, hoaxes created by smooth-talking conmen. But just as many were real, a testament to God's cruelty."

Mr. Balfour coughed gently, before rolling on. He was weak, and obviously did not have many years left on this Earth, but a fire burned in the old man's eyes as he spoke of his bizarre pursuits. The motor on his wheelchair hummed like something alive, malevolent.

Little Sister walked behind Daddy, her shiny black shoes clicking softly on the concrete floor like a clock counting down the seconds until this all came to a head. Meanwhile, Jeremy hummed some tune to himself as if he had seen it all a billion times before.

As they passed those metal shelves, Nick saw hundreds of glass jars of every size and shape. Inside the jars, floating in yellow liquid, were mutated infants—human, bovine, feline, and species he could not identify. Some had more than one head, or flippers for legs, or huge, hydrocephalic skulls. Scattered among these pickled punks were countless manmade cryptids as well, such as a shriveled monkey torso sewn to the bottom half of a fish ("the original Fiji Mermaid, leased for twelve-dollars-and-fifty cents a week by none other than P.T. Barnum himself," Mr. Balfour explained, "even fooled *The New York Sun* at the height of its popularity"). Here and there were stuffed calves, rats, dogs, and lizards with two heads or more. A thousand glassy eyes stared back at Nick as if waiting for the big man to blink so the beasts could attack in unison.

If he weren't so intent on finding Sophie and ending this once and for all, Nick might have been impressed with the crazy old coot's collection. Although he never would have admitted such a thing. Perhaps he would have been gripped, too, by the odd sensation that he shared a sort of *kinship* with the freaks on display.

There was something about this room and everything in it, however, that Nick found...*abandoned*. Neglected and forgotten. Like the inventory for a business that went under years ago, now moldering in the dark with no one around to account for it. The shelves were in disarray—crowded, unorganized, and covered with a thin layer of dust. Many of the stuffed creatures lay on their side, or teetered on the edge of the shelf, about to fall. Most of them were missing some of their fur, or were leaking the sawdust that had replaced their vital organs.

Nick found himself thinking of poor Leon at that moment, and how his friend had been so proud of owning a faded old Widowmaker T-shirt. That was the difference between the have-nots and assholes like this wrinkled fuck in his cash-colored PJs and his motorized wheelchair. Those who had next to nothing appreciated what little they did have. Those who had never known what it was like to go without took their possessions for granted; too much was never enough, and the thrill of the hunt was like a drug to them. They were always searching for something that might impress them even though they had long ago passed the point of being impressed by anything.

Nick fought off the temptation to tear it all down right now, to flood the room with broken glass and formaldehyde and then light a fucking match.

Gotta keep your eye on the prize, he kept reminding himself. *They're gonna take you to Sophie...then and only then you can show your hand and bring this whole fucking thing to the ground...*

Nick stopped in front of a jar containing a plump human fetus with two heads. His own gruesome reflection stared back at him, superimposed over the mutant floating in its liquid. He thought about a pair of conjoined twins born not far from here a half-century ago, twins sold by poverty-stricken parents to a filthy rich pervert who believed that his money gave him the right him to buy anything...even a human being. Maybe that had been the first time Hiram Balfour had purchased a person. Maybe not. But it certainly wasn't the last time.

He wondered if Little Sister and Jeremy shared similar stories. Decided he didn't give a damn if the duo were golems sculpted from the old fart's toe-jam then conjured to life via black magic.

And then Nick found himself pondering who was the real monster here: this wrinkled fiend whose "family" was composed of people he had purchased as part of his peculiar obsession...or a deadbeat father who had ignored his own flesh and blood entirely lest it interfere with his wrestling career. At least those who called Hiram Balfour "Daddy" didn't appear to want for anything. Nick couldn't say the same for his own daughter, whom he had known was damaged from the moment he saw her sitting in that corner booth in Annie's Country Diner (*"somebody who was there for you, did the things fathers are supposed to do, he deserves to be called Daddy, not me"*).

He snapped out of his reverie when he realized Mr. Balfour was rambling on again: "Alas, my fascination with human oddities and aberrations of nature withered and died. I grew bored with it all. And I moved on to...other things."

They came to a heavy metal door painted the same forest-green as Mr. Balfour's pajamas. Little Sister reached into a pocket of her suit, pulled out a small key. She stuck the key in the lock and opened the door.

She flicked another switch, and more fluorescent lights came on... this time exposing a room that stretched into forever. It appeared to be a converted garage, albeit a garage that must have housed thirty or forty vehicles once upon a time. The carpeting was a black-and-gray pattern, like an immense chessboard laid out before Nick and his hosts; it covered the floor as well as the walls. Huge air-conditioning vents blew frigid air down on them as they entered the room.

Balfour said, "As you can see, Mr. Bullman, the last forty years of my life I have been intrigued by the...*cult of celebrity*, if you will. I believe the stars of stage and screen are the freakshow of our modern age. But these 'freaks' have become our gods. Tabloid deities. I suppose what you see before you was a natural progression of my interest in those classic sideshow curiosities. The carnival conmen of yesteryear lured in their marks with promises that they would see 'Bonnie and Clyde's Death Car,' or rust-eaten implements purported to be the tools of history's most notorious murderers. Some men collect comic books or baseball cards; others decorate the walls of their private studies with the severed heads of wild game. This is *my* collection, Mr. Bullman."

"What *is* all of this?" said Nick.

"See for yourself. But, please...I must insist you do not touch anything."

Where the previous room full of pickled punks and stuffed curios had been disorganized, dusty, and abandoned years ago for different pursuits, the collection in this room was obviously a source of great pride for Mr. Balfour. Everything had been painstakingly situated beneath glass cases, or behind velvet ropes, or atop fancy pedestals illuminated by subtle track lighting...like the old man's personal museum...

Here was an orange pill bottle, supposedly one of the very bottles that led to Elvis Presley's demise, according to the brass plaque on its cylindrical base...there, stretched across a wooden frame, was the blanket upon which Marilyn Monroe's body lay the night she died (the square of pink satin was discolored in the center, as if the material were stained to this day by the beauty queen's bodily functions)...atop a thick velvet cushion, sat a pair of round hippie glasses with one shattered lens ("JOHN LENNON/DEC. 8, 1980")...here was a cape that once belonged to TV's first Superman, George Reeves, who had killed himself via a gunshot to the head...there, enclosed within a glass case, was a jar of white greasepaint supposedly worn by Brandon Lee the night he died on the set of *The Crow*...

Everywhere Nick looked was another morbid artifact, memorabilia once owned by a celebrity who was now six feet under.

Against one wall, behind a velvet rope, stood a twisted hunk of metal that resembled nothing so much as a large piece of abstract art. A plaque on a stand a few feet away from it read: "JAMES DEAN/SEPT. 30, 1955."

"Impossible," said Nick. "No way that's the real thing...?"

"Maybe it is, maybe it isn't," Jeremy whispered in his ear. Nick had almost forgotten he was back there. "Daddy believes it's authentic. To him, everything in this room is the real deal. That's all that matters."

Nick knew a lot about the power of belief. It made men do terrible things.

He shook his head as he stood there staring at the wreckage.

The old man rolled past the exhibit, the wheels on his chair leaving faint tracks on the carpet. But then he stopped, turned back toward Nick when he saw what had captured the former wrestler's attention.

"Legend has it that when James Dean introduced himself to Sir Alec Guinness outside of a restaurant in Hollywood, Guinness took one look at Dean's infamous Porsche Spyder and told the young man, 'If you get in that car, you will be found dead in it this time next week.' That conversation occurred one week before Dean's death. For several years after the accident, what remained of the vehicle was displayed publicly. But in 1960, while en route from Florida to Hollywood, the wreckage disappeared. When the trailer reached its destination, it was empty. James Dean's 'Little Bastard' was never seen again."

"Every man has his price," said Nick.

The senior citizen smiled his corpse's smile. "And to some, money is no object."

Nick wondered how many millions the crazy old coot had spent through the years. He stared up at a huge sliver of blackened steel bolted to one wall. According to the plaque beneath it, this was one of the helicopter rotors that had decapitated Vic Morrow during an accident on the set of a 1982 horror film.

"Oh, bullshit," Nick mumbled to himself.

"Quiet, you," said Jeremy.

"Did you know that the Roman guards gambled for possession of Christ's robe when he was crucified?" The old man didn't wait for Nick to answer. "Bystanders ripped a sleeve from President Lincoln's coat after he was assassinated. When the FBI gunned down John Dillinger outside of the Biograph Theatre, spectators dipped their handkerchiefs in the bank-robber's blood."

If he had a point, Mr. Balfour explained it no further. At last, he rolled to a stop. He turned in his chair to face Nick.

They had come to the far end of the room. Against that wall stood a tall, thin wooden shelf. Sitting on the shelf at Nick's eye-level, backlit by a glowing green light, was a glass jar filled with clear liquid.

Something else was in the jar, too.

"NICHOLAS JAMES BULLMAN," read the shiny gold plaque

beneath it, "A.K.A 'THE WIDOWMAKER'."

"What the fuck?" said Nick.

It took him several seconds to figure out what he was looking at.

After all, it had been three long years since the last time he laid eyes on it.

†

When the truth finally hit him—like a sledgehammer upside the head—Nick stumbled backward, crashing into Jeremy behind him.

"I know this must be a shock," said Mr. Balfour.

Nick didn't hear him. His pulse pounded in his ears like a tympani drum.

"You...sent them. Rebel Yell and One-Arm. You *sent them...*"

"I assure you," said the old man, "I know no one by those names."

"Liar! You hired them! God damn you."

Nick took a step toward the old man, his hands balled into fists, but Little Sister stepped between them.

Balfour said, "I have no reason to lie to you. I acquired this particular specimen...after. I heard about what happened that night in Amarillo, and my associates moved quickly. The cost, of course, was extravagant. But then, nothing in my collection has ever been cheap."

Nick's guts roiled as he stared at it...at that rubbery thing stretched taut between two vertical wire rods inside its green-glowing canister...like a silently-screaming phantasm trapped between the dimensions of the living and the dead.

His face. His fucking *face.*

He could even see a hint of stubble along its bottom half, where he had been in need of a shave the last time he had worn it. A few tiny bubbles were trapped within the hairs.

"They could have *saved* it. They could have sewed it back on. But they never found it. Because you paid...you twisted son of a bitch...you paid someone to—"

"If it is any consolation," said Mr. Balfour, "I have taken very good care of my investment. I cherish it so."

"Ah," said Nick. "That makes it all better, then."

"At one time, it was my most prized possession."

Nick's chest heaved in and out. Tears of rage filled his eyes. He could barely hold himself back. He imagined picking up the old man—

wheelchair and all—and heaving him across the room as if he weighed nothing. But he was close...*so close*...for all he knew, Sophie was within shouting distance right now...

"Speaking of my most prized possession," the old man said, almost as if he were reading Nick's mind, "please take us to Sophie's room now. Little Sister, Jeremy...I think it is time Mr. Bullman met his granddaughter."

†

They exited Balfour's "museum" through a side door. Crossed through an atrium filled with azalea bushes and dogwood trees. A stone angel watched them pass. Directly overhead, visible through a domed skylight, lurked a bright full moon.

Then they were inside again. At the end of another short hallway was a door that looked as if it had been painted recently. Hot pink.

"After you," said Mr. Balfour.

Little Sister reached into her pocket for another key. She handed it to Nick, and gestured for him to lead the way.

The big man stepped forward, his heart thudding in his chest.

He stuck the key in the lock and turned it.

He opened the door.

The teenager lay on her side on a huge canopy bed, surrounded by pink. Pink blankets, pink pillows, pink wallpaper on all four sides of her. The only light in the room came from a small pink lamp with a pink lampshade, sitting on a pink nightstand. She was surrounded by chubby teddy bears and dolls with frilly pink dresses. It was as if this room had been decorated specifically for a little girl, and filled with everything a child could ask for...if the child who occupied these quarters were seven instead of fourteen.

Nick grew lightheaded when he saw his granddaughter for the first time.

She was the most beautiful thing he had ever seen.

Her skin was pale. She looked ten or fifteen pounds skinnier than any pictures he had seen of her, and there were dark bags under her eyes, as if living in captivity had taken its toll on her body. Her forehead was shiny with sweat. Her dark, curly hair was wet as if she had taken a shower right before bed. As she slept, one of her nostrils whistled softly. She wore only a thin pink nightshirt with the words DADDY'S GIRL across the chest; it had ridden up on her bottom to expose her thin white panties.

"Is she okay?" Nick asked. "What's wrong with her?"

"Nothing's wrong with her," said Little Sister. "She has been treated like a princess from the moment she first arrived here."

Nick couldn't help sensing something *envious* in her tone. As if she had once been Daddy's favorite but those days were a distant memory, and she wasn't happy about that at all.

"Is she on something?"

"Of course not," said Jeremy, with a condescending chuckle that made Nick want to turn and rip out his stomach through his mouth. "It's one o' clock in the morning. She's sleeping."

Nick stood there for at least another minute, staring at his granddaughter.

Finally, he swallowed a lump in his throat, and asked the old man, "Why? You already had my...my face. So...why Sophie? Why did you have to take her?"

"She is your blood, Mr. Bullman. You were a celebrity, once upon a time. Your story is a fascinating one. You suffered a terrible tragedy. That made Sophie a fine addition to my collection. The finest."

A foul taste filled Nick's mouth. "It wasn't just about that, though. What did you plan to *do* with her?"

Daddy likes kids...always has...and she was just his type...

Sophie stirred then. She coughed gently, rubbed at her eyes. Sat up in bed.

Her jaw dropped when she saw Nick standing there.

"You. Oh my...it's you."

"Hello, Sophie," said Nick. "Do you know who I am?"

"Of course I do. You're my grandfather."

"That's right, baby." His voice cracked. Tears blurred his vision. "I'm here now, Sophie. Everything's gonna be okay."

She ran to him, fell into his arms. No one tried to stop her.

She smelled like strawberry-scented shampoo. To Nick, it was the greatest smell in the world.

He cleared his throat, stepped back. His big hands gripped his granddaughter's shoulders as he looked into her bright blue eyes—eyes that looked just like his own.

It was time to show his ace in the hole.

Softly, he said, "Sophie? I need to ask you something. I don't want to know, but I *need* to know…"

"What?"

"Did he touch you?"

Her bottom lip quivered. A tear trickled down her cheek.

"He tried." She shot Little Sister a look of hatred. "*She* held me down. They took pictures. But he couldn't do what he wanted to do. He got mad. He called me names, and he gave up."

"Christ," said Nick, hanging his head. "I'm sorry, honey. I'm so sorry…"

"It is a weakness of mine, I admit," said Mr. Balfour. "I do love children so."

"Sick *fuck*," Nick growled at the old man.

"Watch it," said Little Sister.

Nick ignored her. He kissed Sophie on her sweaty forehead and said, "Thank you for telling me that, baby. I needed to hear it. So I could be sure that what I'm about to do is the right thing…"

Little Sister and Jeremy exchanged puzzled looks. Mr. Balfour smiled up at Nick, as if he thought the big man might be about to offer him another piece of his body for his collection.

"You people are the monsters here," said Nick. "*You're* the ugly ones."

He shoved Sophie back then—perhaps a bit too roughly, but he couldn't take any chances—and he pulled the gun from beneath his shirt.

It was a gold-plated Beretta. Taken from a man who called himself Coko Puff. At the time, he hadn't been sure why he took it with him. *Just in case* had seemed as good a reason as any. The weapon had been hidden in the waistline of his pants ever since he left the dealer's house. He had almost pulled it at the 'Rim, but he had known then that if he killed the only people who could lead him to Sophie, he might never find her. Allowing the siblings to take him, on their terms, was the only way he would find his granddaughter.

His patience had paid off.

"Jeremy, you *idiot!*" Little Sister shouted. "You didn't *search* him?"

Jeremy went for his own gun, in his jacket.

He was fast. Nick hadn't expected him to be so fast. He fired once, and his shot caught Nick in his right thigh.

Nick grunted, stumbled back, and pulled the Beretta's trigger twice.

Crimson blossoms opened up in Jeremy's chest. The younger man dropped to his knees, and then his body hit the floor face-first.

Little Sister screamed—a hoarse, masculine roar. She went for Jeremy's pistol.

Nick fired again.

Blood spurted from the woman's throat, and she went down on top of her brother.

"No!" Mr. Balfour cried. "What have you done? *What have you done?*"

The old man fumbled around on his wheelchair. Found what he was looking for after a few seconds. He brought out his own weapon now, from a pocket under one of the armrests—a small, antique-looking handgun.

"Bastard," he hissed at Nick, as he pulled back the hammer.

Nick thought about it for maybe half a second, then shot the old man in the chest.

Balfour arched his back as if he were merely straining to let out a dusty old-man fart. Then his body went slack. His chin touched his chest. He died without another sound.

Sophie wrapped her arms around Nick from behind. He flinched.

Nick held her in one arm, while his other hand went to his thigh. Blood spurted out of the wound, through his fingers. He staggered, crashed into the wall, but somehow stayed on his feet.

"Are you okay?" she asked him.

"I'll be okay," he said, although he wasn't entirely sure yet. "Do you know your way around this place?"

"A little," she replied. "But it's really big. They hardly ever let me out of my room."

"That's fine. I don't even know where we are." He nodded toward Jeremy's corpse. "He has a cellphone in his jacket. I'm gonna use it to call 911. They'll be able to find us."

He limped over to the dead man, started searching for the phone. Sophie held onto his shirttail the whole way, as if she would never let him out of her sight.

"By the way," she said, "it's a pleasure to finally meet you, Grandpa."

In spite of the pain in his thigh, a crooked grin stretched across Nick's disfigured face.

"Better late than never, right? It's a pleasure to meet you too, sweetheart."

One month later...

After it was over, and the Polk County Sheriff's Department had concluded its investigation, the funeral home placed notices in several newspapers, searching for family to claim Leon Purdy's remains. Their efforts were futile. He would soon be cremated, and his ashes buried in a local Potter's Field.

That didn't sit well with the man once known as the Widowmaker. His number one fan deserved better.

†

He closed out all of his bank accounts, which proved more depressing than anything. But every little bit would help.

When that was done, he headed across town to the auto shop where his Bronco had been sitting since its release from police custody.

†

The mechanic was a broad-shouldered fellow in his mid-sixties with a purple birthmark over half his face. EZRA, read the name on his filthy coveralls.

"You're the wrestler, ain'tcha? Me and my wife, God rest her soul, we used to watch you all the time. What can I do you for, Mr. Bullman?"

"I'm here for the Bronco," said Nick. "What's the damage?"

"Afraid it's gonna cost you more to fix her up than she's worth. You're lookin' at a whole new engine block, for starters."

"Shit," said Nick.

"You got other options."

"I'm listening."

"I could buy her off of you, for parts. Few hundred bucks is all I could do. But it's better than nothin'."

"What the hell. Let's do it."

†

"How may I help you today?" asked the funeral director, a chubby young man with fiery red hair.

"I'm here for Leon Purdy. I'd like to buy him a plot. And a nice stone."

"I can certainly take care of that for you. Let's talk about what you would like engraved upon his marker. This will serve your friend's memory well, sir."

"Great," said Nick.

He pulled out his wallet.

When that was done, he took a few minutes to visit Melissa's mama's grave. He laid down the bouquet of daffodils he had brought, but he didn't say anything. He just stood there in solemn meditation, leaning on his cane, in the cool late-summer drizzle.

†

Nick shook Sheriff Mackey's hand, thanked him for the ride. The two men had actually started to become good friends these last few weeks.

He dabbed at his leaking right eye, adjusted his sunglasses before carefully climbing out of the patrol car.

The sheriff pulled away from the curb with a brief *bloop-whoop* of his siren.

Thirty seconds later, they caught him walking through the front door of the Polk County Rec Center, attacked Nick Bullman before the door had closed all the way behind him...

†

Like vultures descending upon carrion prey, they surrounded him. Their numbers overwhelmed him.

They thrust their Sharpies at him along with dog-eared copies of old wrestling zines, faded pin-ups, and out-of-print VHS covers. The group consisted of four boys no older than ten or eleven; a lanky teenage guy with terrible acne, and an obese middle-aged couple wearing matching THE WIDOWMAKER ATE MY SOUL!!! T-shirts.

Nick felt a twinge of claustrophobia as they invaded his personal space. But he signed what they shoved in front of him. He asked the teenager with bad acne where in the world had he found an unopened, mint-condition 'Maker action figure (the original one with the inverted-cross makeup that had quickly been discontinued). The youth stuttered something about "sniping on ebay." Nick didn't have a clue what that meant, but he was humbled nonetheless.

He remembered a time when he had loved every second of this. Realized he still dug it quite a bit. It had been years since anyone wanted to approach him, or since he wanted to be approached.

He thanked them all for coming out. Promised he would chat some more with every single one of them, once he got settled in.

He hobbled toward the gymnasium, where a number of folding tables and chairs had been set up for today's event. A giant banner hung along one wall, featuring a sloppy photo collage of five sweaty wrestlers flexing and snarling in colorful spandex. Each was a performer that had been at the top of the wrestling hierarchy once upon a time. But, whether thanks to the fickleness of fans eternally obsessed with the "next big thing" or due to their own bad decisions, most of them had not appeared on TV for the better part of a decade.

TODAY ONLY:
MEET YOUR FAVORITE WRESTLING LEGENDS!

BIG JIM BROGAN, JR.
NICK "THE WIDOWMACKER" BULLMEN
PAUL "BLACK SAMSON" SHERMAN
TEDDY "THE BEAR" GORGINO
SLICK RICK MONAVIE

4:30–6:30 PM

(* see celebs for pricing/merchandise *)

Nick didn't mind that they had grossly misspelled his name. He barely even noticed, in fact.

He bent to clear the doorway, and as he entered the gym he removed his dark glasses, searching for the two people who had recently stolen his heart.

He spotted them on the opposite side of the gym, standing beneath a folded-up basketball goal. Melissa and Sophie waved at him. The teen hopped up and down like a child half her age, as if she couldn't wait to throw her arms around him. She wore black track-pants that matched his own and a purple T-shirt sporting the Widowmaker's old logo. Nick smiled crookedly. He was glad to see that she had put on a few pounds over the last few days, and gained some color back in her face. Soon she would look no different from any normal fourteen-year-old, one who hadn't recently suffered a terrifying ordeal.

He made his way through the crowd. Embraced them both.

"How are my two favorite ladies? Love the shirt, Soph."

His granddaughter beamed up at him.

"You look a little nervous," said Melissa.

"I didn't think that was possible. I make *other* people nervous, remember?" He bared his teeth, growled like a B-movie monster.

His daughter slapped him lightly on the arm.

"Been a long time since I've done something like this," he said. "But it's cool."

"It's very cool," said Sophie, unable to take her eyes off of him.

"What about you, kiddo? How are you holding up?"

"I'm fine," she said. "It gets easier every day."

"Yeah," he said. "It does."

He pulled her close, kissed the top of her head.

They had spent a lot of time together in the weeks since Nick rescued his granddaughter from Hiram Balfour's insanity. He had learned so much about her, and he couldn't wait to learn even more. Perhaps the thing that blew his mind the most was when Sophie told him that she had tried to contact him on more than one occasion over the last couple of years. She had used his old e-mail address as well as a "snail mail addy" she'd found when she "Googled" him, but eventually she had given up when her letters bounced back as undeliverable or she got no response at all. She told him over a picnic lunch in Washington Park that she wanted to be a journalist, and it was her dream to one day write a book about the Global Wrestling Association's most infamous monster heel.

She loved cheesy horror movies, the poetry of Carl Sandburg, coffee ice cream, *Family Guy*, Minecraft, and loud rock n' roll (not to mention "some of those classic blues guys," which made her granddad adore her even more). And lasagna. The kid *really* loved lasagna.

The previous weekend they had gone to see the new Batman flick, and Nick couldn't remember the last time he'd had so much fun. But today, here at the rec center, marked the first time he had seen Melissa or Sophie since their trip to the movies. He had been very busy the past few days. Not in the same way he had been "too busy" for his daughter when she was growing up—this time, the things that preoccupied Nick were investments in their future. A future together...

For the first time in over thirty years, Nick was once again a citizen of Midnight, North Carolina. He had signed a twelve-month lease on a doublewide in a quiet mobile home park not far from Melissa's apartment. He had even found a job here. Turned out one of his favorite places in the world when he was a kid, Annie's Country Diner, was in dire need of a third-shift short-order cook. He was slow right now, hobbling around on his cane, but so was business at that time of night. He didn't need to run races, his employer assured him, as long as he could whip up a mean double cheeseburger with a side of chili-and-cheese fries.

More fans were filing into the rec center now, although the event wasn't scheduled to begin for another forty minutes. It was here, Sheriff Mackey had informed Nick, that hundreds of volunteers had set up a temporary call-center in the first few days following Sophie's disappearance. As he walked through the gym, Nick passed an old MISSING poster taped to the wall. He tore it down, crumpled it into a ball and tossed it at a nearby wastebasket. It felt good, even though he missed by a mile.

Beyond the throng Nick glimpsed a group of muscle-bound men entering the building, towering over everyone else. He recognized their faces right away even though he hadn't seen them in years. One, a Native American fellow Nick had known since he was Melissa's age, threw up a giant hand when their eyes met across the gym. Nick returned the gesture. Soon they would all exchange hugs and firm handshakes. He looked forward to catching up with his old friends, maybe trading a few war stories.

Most importantly, he looked forward to introducing them to his family. It had been a long time coming.

A lady in a loud yellow pantsuit hurried into the gym then, her heels click-clacking on the hardwood floor. A frazzled-looking cameraman followed in her wake, nearly tripping over his own feet as he tried to keep up with her. NEWS 13, read the logo on the side of his camera.

They made a beeline for Nick.

"Here we go again," said Sophie. "My granddad, the rock star..."

"I don't know about that," said Nick. "They probably want to talk to *you*."

But then he closed his eyes, tilted his head back, played a few furious licks on his cane as if it were an electric guitar.

Sophie's giggles echoed through the gym.

He could feel everyone in the room staring at him. Just like always.

But these days Nick Bullman didn't mind at all.

JAMES NEWMAN lives in the mountains of North Carolina with his wife and their two sons. His published works include the novels *Midnight Rain*, *Animosity*, and *Ugly As Sin*, the short-story collection *People Are Strange*, and the novellas *The Forum*, *Olden*, and *Odd Man Out*. When he's not writing, James enjoys watching college basketball and listening to loud rock n' roll . . . often at the same time.

Catch up with James online at http://www.james-newman.com.

WARNING!

The following Q&A contains major spoilers for *Ugly As Sin*. If you skipped to this part before reading the novel, the author strongly suggests you turn back now. So does the interviewee...and you wouldn't want to argue with the Widowmaker, would you?

MORE THAN A
MONSTER

A CHAT WITH NICK BULLMAN

BY ANDREW HOLLAND

Once upon a time, he was the skull-faced fiend everyone loved to hate. As the Global Wrestling Association's reviled "Widowmaker," he inflicted maximum pain upon his opponents just because he liked hurting others. Even death could not keep him down; he fought the Grim Reaper and won (in fact, die-hard fans will recall that the Reaper suffered not only broken bones but humiliation in front of millions following the encounter, when he was disrobed on live television). His legendary feuds with Big Bubba Bad-Ass brought ratings to the GWA the likes of which the franchise had never seen before. He is a six-time Hardcore Champion, a six-time International Champion, and a six-time World Heavyweight Champion (put those numbers together, and they make perfect sense...after all, we are talking about the self-proclaimed "Son of Eternal Darkness", who once sold his soul to keep winning matches).

But what about the *real* Nick Bullman?

I've known Nick for almost twenty years now. The first time I met him, we sat side-by-side, signing autographs at a popular horror convention in New Jersey (Nick had recently starred in the slasher flick *Night of the Berzerker*, and my novelization of the same was hot off the press). The thing I recall most vividly about that day is how *small* I felt, sitting there in his shadow, as if the big man blocked out the sun itself. His deep voice was intimidating at first, like the rumbling growl of a beast when it's backed into a corner. But I found him to be personable, if a bit reserved.

Back then, I was glad he wasn't my enemy. These days, I am proud to call him my friend.

I'm here to tell you that Nick Bullman is so much more than the sadistic persona he portrayed for three decades. He is anything *but* a monster (although, in his self-deprecating way, he is quick to insist that he looks like one). He is a father. A grandfather. He is a man who has known his share of pain—*real* pain—after an encounter with two psychotic fans left him disfigured. But in the end his trials have made him a better person.

You've heard all the clichés: "Beauty is in the eye of the beholder." "It's what's on the inside that counts."

Not too long ago, it would have been *ground glass* in the eyes of the beholder. What's on the inside would have been *outside* (of his enemies' bodies). Thanks to the Widowmaker.

People can change, though. Nick Bullman is living proof of that.

But don't take my word for it...

Andrew Holland: How are you, Nick?

Nick Bullman: I'm good, Andy.

AH: Your granddaughter is home safe and sound, and it's all because of you. How does that feel?

NB: You wanna know the truth, I'm still adjusting to the news that I'm a grandfather. Even after everything that happened, I'm having a hell of a time wrapping my head around it. It doesn't feel real, I guess 'cause I never had time to let it sink in before things got crazy with the Charlies, Jeremy and Little Sister, and that sick old bastard Balfour.

As for all this "hero" crap the press has been throwing around...whatever, man. I did what I had to do, when Melissa needed me. For once in my life, I decided it was time to nut up and act like a father.

AH: How are Melissa and Sophie holding up?

NB: Both of them are still having nightmares. Melissa says she dreams at least twice a week that Sophie's gone missing again, and the kid keeps waking up in the middle of the night thinking she sees Little Sister standing over her, or Balfour's face staring through

her bedroom window. We're all just taking it day by day. Sophie's seeing a therapist. I think that's helped her a lot.

AH: And yourself? What are you up to these days, Nick?

NB: I'm just trying to spend as much time with my girls as possible. Got a job flipping burgers down at Annie's Country Diner. It's boring as shit, but it pays the bills. And who says *boring* has to be a bad thing? Better than waking up in the middle of the night with a gun in your face, or getting a needle full of horse tranquilizer jabbed into your neck.

AH: After thirty-plus years in show business, traveling all over the world, what's left to do that Nick Bullman hasn't done already?

NB: Like I said, all I wanna do from here on out is keep learning how to be a good father. I've got thirty years to make up for. It won't be easy, but I'm gonna try my best. I'm in this for the long haul, man.

AH: What do you miss most about professional wrestling? The least?

NB: There was nothing in the world like the roar of the crowd. Heel or babyface [**ed.** wrestling jargon for "bad guy" or "good guy," respectively], it didn't matter. The pop [**ed.** emphatic audience reaction] was like a drug. I dreamed of being a superstar ever since I was a kid. I achieved that dream. I'd be lying if I said I don't miss it now and then.

I don't miss what the Biz does to your body over time. You can't put flesh and bone through hell like that, every night for thirty years, without causing permanent damage. When we're young and dumb we think we're invincible. On rainy days this bum knee of mine hurts so bad I wanna chop off my whole damn leg and be done with it.

AH: I've heard rumors of a biopic. What's up with that? And who would get your vote to play "The Widowmaker" on the silver screen?

NB: I've been contacted [about it] more than once. Who knows. Call me a whore, but I wouldn't turn them away if the money was right. I could use a new truck. The last one had to be put out of its misery.

Who'd play me? It's not something I've given much thought. It's Hollywood, so they're bound to screw it up if it happens. All I know is, any dude who plays Nick Bullman better be ready to spend some time in the makeup chair.

AH: Switching gears for a moment…there was a time, shortly after you first returned to Midnight, when your relationship with Sheriff Kyle Mackey was rather tense. I understand that's a thing of the past?

NB: Mackey's a good man. We still do a bit of verbal sparring now and then, but it's all in fun. We respect one another a great deal. He had a lot to do with keeping the D.A. off my ass after what went down at Balfour's house. There was an investigation—the D.A. didn't like the fact that I had that drug dealer's gun on me, and for a while it looked like he was gonna use the gun to prove I had "premeditated" something—but in the end they called it self-defense. 'Cause that's what it was. The only thing I premeditated was going to get my granddaughter.

AH: You recently shared something with me that you thought your fans would like to know…a juicy bit of news regarding your former employer, Lance K. McDougal III? Can you talk about that?

NB: Gladly. Last month, the Global Wrestling Association's C.E.O. was arrested for securities fraud and obstruction of justice. Insider trading stuff. I hear he's facing up to three years behind bars. But it gets better. I just found out that the prick's been hit with a class-action lawsuit by no less than a dozen young ladies on his payroll. Sexual harassment.

Karma is a bitch.

AH: Last but certainly not least, anything you'd like to say about Leon? Do you miss him?

NB: Sure. I didn't know him for long. But he got murdered trying to help me. I'll never forget my "number one fan." I'd like to think I could have helped him get clean. I know the little freak would have done anything to make me happy. That would have made me happy.

AH: Nick, I want to thank you for taking the time to chat with me today. Always a pleasure.

NB: Pleasure's all mine, Andy. There's so much more I have to tell you, though. You thought the stuff with Balfour was insane? Wait till you hear about the KKK shitheads, and this crazy-ass cult I pissed off without even trying too hard...

AH: I can't wait to hear about this!

NB: Problem is, my contract with James [Newman] says I can't talk about it in print until it hits his next book.

AH: Damn it, man. That was just wrong.

NB: I said I couldn't talk about it in print. But you're a professional, I figure you know how to keep your trap shut. I don't see any reason why we couldn't wrap this up right now, and I'll tell you all about it over a beer.

AH: Make it more than one. Let me buy, and you've got yourself a deal.

NB: My turn to ask you a question, Andy...why the hell are we still sitting here?

Andrew Holland
Midnight, North Carolina
August 1, 2013

Andrew Holland is the bestselling author of *Wolf Moon*, *Slow Burn*, and *House On Harding Street*. He lives in eastern Tennessee with his daughter Samantha and a general distrust of humanity.

Holland recently survived a real life horror story of his own, which you can read all about in the book *Animosity* (by James Newman).

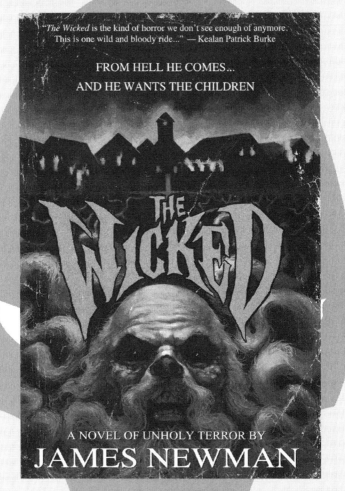